LADY GUNSMITH

10

Roxy Doyle Meets an Angel

Books by J.R. Roberts
(Robert J. Randisi)

Lady Gunsmith series
The Legend of Roxy Doyle
The Three Graves of Roxy Doyle
Roxy Doyle and The Shanghai Saloon
Roxy Doyle and The Traveling Circus Show
The Portrait of Gavin Doyle
Roxy Doyle and the Desperate Housewife
Roxy Doyle and the James Boys
Roxy Doyle and the Silver Queen
Roxy Doyle and the Lady Executioner
Roxy Doyle Meets an Angel

The Gunsmith series

Gunsmith Giant series

Angel Eyes series

Tracker series

Mountain Jack Pike series

For more information visit:
www.SpeakingVolumes.us

LADY GUNSMITH

10

Roxy Doyle Meets an Angel

J.R. Roberts

SPEAKING VOLUMES, LLC
NAPLES, FLORIDA
2022

Roxy Doyle Meets an Angel

ISBN 978-1-64540-349-4

Chapter One

Roxy Doyle was used to eyes following her when she rode into a town—especially the men's. But she was determined to live her life in the open, and not in hiding. That was why she never hid her flaming red hair beneath a hat. And the few times she felt it necessary to hide her curves, she did so beneath a serape.

But today she was on display for all to see. The women frowned when they saw her riding in, despite the fact that she was pretty grimy from four days in the saddle. After she boarded her horse, and got a hotel room, the next thing she wanted—even before a meal—was a bath.

Of the three hotels in the Wyoming town of Coverton, the Cedar House was the largest. Still, when Roxy asked about a bath when she checked in, she was told the hotel didn't have one.

"The best place would be the barber shop across the street. He's got two tubs in the back."

"The barber shop?"

"Sorry, Ma'am."

"I'll make do. Thanks."

She stowed her saddlebags and rifle in her room, then left the hotel and crossed to the barber shop. When she entered, she became the immediate center of attention. The barber, a man in the chair, and the men waiting all stared at her.

"Uh, Ma'am," the barber said, "I'm afraid I don't do ladies hair."

"That's all right," she said. "I heard you have bath-tubs."

"Oh, yes, Ma'am," the barber said. "Two in the back."

"Hot water?"

"Oh, yes. Ma'am."

"Then I'd like a bath, please."

"Yes, Ma'am." He turned his head. "Jason!"

A boy of about ten came running in from the back.

"The lady wants a hot bath," the barber said, "Fill the tub for her."

"Yes, Mr. Holden." The boy looked at Roxy. "This way, Ma'am."

"I'll follow you."

He led her down a hall, and before they reached the door at the end, he turned and said, "Wow, Miss, you're pretty."

"Thank you, Jason," she said. "You should see me when I'm clean."

"Yes, ma'am," he said, enthusiastically.

When they reached the end of the hall she saw two doors.

"You can wait in there," he said, pointing to one. "There are clean towels. I'll knock on the door from the other room when your bath is ready."

"Thank you, Jason."

She opened the door and found herself in a room with one empty bathtub. She assumed the connecting door led to the other tub, which was being filled by Jason.

She removed her clothing and wrapped herself in one of the towels. It left her exposed from the top of her thighs down. That done she sat and waited for a knock on the connecting door. When it came she stood, opened the door and walked in, carrying her clothes. The room was identical to the other one, only this tub was filled with steamy hot water. She laid her clothes on a chair, and her gunbelt on top of them, within easy reach.

"Can I do anythin' else for you, Ma'am?" Jason asked. His eyes were wide as he stared at her thighs and legs.

"How old are you, Jason?" she asked.

"I'm thirteen."

"You're small for your age."

He bowed his head.

"I know."

"There's nothing else you can do for me," she told him. "Thanks."

"Yes, Ma'am."

Reluctantly, he took his eyes from her and left the room. She laughed to herself. She had suspected he was older than he looked because of the bulge in his trousers while he stared at her.

She went to the tub, dropped the towel to the floor, then stepped in. She grabbed the soap and began forming suds in her hands, then rubbed them on her legs and arms. Next, she worked on her torso and finished by washing her hair, face and neck, then settled back to relax a bit in the heated water . . .

***

When the water started to get tepid, she stood up, stepped out and dried off. Then she went to the connect-ing door and re-entered the other room, carrying her clothes and gunbelt. There she dressed, strapped on her gun and walked to the front of the barber shop.

Chapter Two

As soon as she entered, she knew something was wrong. There was only the barber and one customer in his chair. The others were gone. The barber seemed very nervous.

"How much do I owe you for the bath?" she asked.

"Oh, uh, a dollar should do it."

She took the money out and held it out to him. She wanted to see him reach for it and, sure enough, his hand was shaking. A close look at the man in the chair revealed a bulge beneath the cloth. She was used to seeing men with bulges, and she could always tell a penis from a gun.

This was a gun.

The barber took the dollar and backed up to his chair. However, he made no move to cut the man's hair. The man hadn't made a move either, so she assumed he was going to wait for her to head for the door and shoot her in the back.

She decided not to give him a chance. Drawing her gun quickly she pointed it at him and the barber.

"Take that cloth off him," she told the barber.

"Yes, Ma'am."

He grabbed the edge and slowly slid it off, revealing the man to be sitting with a gun in his hand.

"You were going to wait for me to walk out the door and then shoot me, right?"

"Uh—"

"I got a better idea," she said. "Shoot me now."

The man licked his lips and again said, "Uh—"

"If you're not going to use it, drop the gun to the floor."

He opened his hand and let the pistol slide from his lap.

"What's this about?" she asked.

He licked his lips again.

"Price," he said, "a price on your head."

"On *my* head?" she asked. "What for? From who?"

"Don't know," he said. "I only know there's five thousand dollars on your head."

"Dead or alive?" she asked.

He shook his head.

"Dead," he said.

"Well," she said, "if you don't want to die, I wouldn't move from that chair."

"Don't worry, I won't."

She looked at the window.

"Are there others out there?" she asked. "Your friends?"

"Friends?"

"The ones who were waiting for you to get your hair cut," she said.

"Oh, yeah, well, uh—"

She started for the door. At that point, Jason came running in.

"Don't go out there!" he yelled.

"What'd you see, Jason?"

"Three of 'em," he said. "They're waitin' across the street to ambush you."

"Point them out, Jason."

He started for the door, but she grabbed him.

"From here."

He stopped, then pointed. "There, there and there."

"Pistols or rifles?"

"One with a pistol, there, and two with rifles, there."

"All right," she said. "Stay where you are."

"I could go for the sheriff!"

"Just stay in here," she said. "I might send you for the sheriff after." She pointed to the gun on the floor. "Pick that up. If he moves from that chair, shoot him. Can you do that?"

"Yes, Ma'am!" Jason eagerly picked up the gun and pointed it at the man in the chair.

"The same for the barber, here."

7

"That's Mr. Holden," Jason said. "He wouldn't try to shoot you."

"I'll take your word for it, Jason."

She moved toward the door.

"Ain't you gonna take out your gun?" Jason called after her.

"I will, when I need it," she assured him.

She went to the doorway, stood there and looked out. If they were hiding from her, then none of them thought they were good enough to face her.

She looked across the street at the three locations Jason had indicated, saw two of the three men. She kept her eyes on them as she stepped out. He could pull the trigger. She drew and fired. The bullet took him square in the chest. The second man stood with his rifle and fell victim to the same fate. He dropped his rifle as her bullet struck him.

She waited for the third man to make a move, either to fire his weapon, or run. She wanted one of them alive, in case he had the answers to her questions.

"Throw away your gun and step out!" she called.

There was no response. Had he already hightailed it? Men were running toward the activity. She turned and went back into the barber shop.

"Two of your friends are dead," she told the man in the chair. "You're going to come out and look at them and tell me who the third man is."

"Should I get the sheriff?" Jason asked.

She looked at the boy, took the gun from him and said, "I'm sure he's already on his way."

Chapter Three

The first man through the door of the barber shop was wearing a sheriff's badge. He was medium height, thick in the middle and middle-aged.

"I'm Sheriff Cal Evers," the man said. "What happened here?"

"I just arrived in town and came in for a bath," Roxy told him. "This fellow and his friends decided they wanted to kill me."

The sheriff looked at the man in the chair.

"Conroy, isn't it?"

"Yeah, sheriff."

"You know him?" Roxy asked.

"He works on the Bar-V ranch, outside of town."

"And the men outside?"

"They're probably also ranch hands." Evers rubbed his jaw. "Why would a bunch of ranch hands decide to kill you if you just arrived?"

"This one said there's a price on my head."

"Is there?"

"Not that I know of."

"What's your name?"

"Roxy Doyle."

"That's not her name," Conroy said. "She's Liz Archer."

"Archer?" the lawman repeated.

"That's what James said," Conroy replied. "He said he recognized her."

"Is James one of the men I killed?" Roxy asked.

"I don't know," the sheriff said. "Let's take him outside and find out."

Conroy finally got out of the chair and stretched.

"Let's go."

Roxy, the sheriff and Conroy walked outside. There were some men picking the bodies up from the street.

"Hold on there," the sheriff called. "We want to take a look."

He walked over to the bodies with Roxy and Conroy.

"So?" the sheriff said to Conroy.

"That's Foster," Conroy said, pointing to one man, and then "that's Eagan," pointing to the other.

"Then James got away," Roxy said. "Where can I find him?"

"Take it easy," the lawman said. "We still have to talk, Miss Doyle, or Archer, or whoever you are. Let's go to my office."

"What about me?" Conroy asked.

"He didn't do anythin', did he?" Sheriff Evers asked her.

11

"Only because I got the drop on him first," she said. "He had a gun hidden, waiting for me to turn my back."

"You come to my office, too," Evers said. "I don't want you warning James."

They all walked to the sheriff's office while the bodies were removed from the street.

"Wait here," he said to Roxy. "I'll put him in a cell."

"What for?" Conroy demanded. "I didn't do nothin'."

"You were gonna try and kill this lady, whatever her name is," Evers said. "Now move!"

He walked the man into the cell block and Roxy heard a door open and close. Then the sheriff returned.

"Let's sit," he said, and seated himself behind his desk.

There was a chair in front of the desk, so Roxy lowered herself onto it.

"Let's start with your name."

"I told you," she said, "Roxy Doyle."

"And what are you doin' in town?"

"Passing through," she said. "I've been in the saddle four days and needed a bath."

"And you never saw any of these men before?" he asked.

"No."

"What about this other name?" Evers asked. "Liz Archer?"

"I never heard of her," Roxy said.

"I have," the sheriff said. "She's also known as Angel Eyes. She's quite a hand with a gun."

"Why would those men think I was her?" Roxy asked. "Do we look alike?"

"Well," Evers said, "you're both beautiful, and good with a gun. You *are* known as Lady Gunsmith, aren't you?"

"I am."

"But you have red hair and she has blonde," Evers said.

"So you think they thought I changed my hair color?"

"I'll know that when I find this fella James. I'm goin' out to the Bar-V tomorrow."

"You mind if I go along?"

"I don't mind, at all," the lawman said. "Meet me out front at nine a.m."

"I'll be there," she said.

"If I was you, I'd be real careful," the lawman said. "If these men mistook you for someone else, it could happen again."

"Thanks, I'll do that," she said. "Anything else?"

"No," he said, "we can talk again as we ride to the Bar-V," he said.

"That suits me," she said, standing. "Can you direct me to a good steak?"

"That I can do."

Chapter Four

Roxy found the steak edible. Next time she would ask someone for advice about where to get a better one. After eating, she decided not to risk being mistaken for Liz Archer again, so instead of going to a saloon, she went to her room.

She had breakfast the next morning in the hotel, then went to the sheriff's office with her horse. She saw a saddled horse outside.

"There you are," Evers said. "I was gettin' ready to go."

"I'm ready," Roxy said. "How far to the Bar-V?"

"About ten miles outside of town. Shouldn't take us that long."

They went outside and mounted their horses.

***

As the sheriff had said, the ride out to the ranch didn't take long. The set-up was impressive, with a two-story house, a large barn and two corrals. As they rode to the house, ranch hands turned to watch them.

They had talked during the ride out, so Roxy knew the Bar-V was owned by a man named Victor Newport. The foreman's name was Dave Jesse.

They dismounted and looked around. A tall, rangy man in his late thirties was approaching them. Roxy made notice of the fact he was ruggedly good looking.

"Sheriff," the man said.

"Dave," Evers replied. "This is Roxy Doyle. We'd like to see Mr. Newport."

"He's inside," Jesse said, speaking to the sheriff, but looking at Roxy. "I'm sure he'll have time for you. Follow me."

He led them up the steps and through the front door. They came to a large staircase, with doors to the right and left.

"He should be in here," Jesse said, leading them right.

As they entered the room, a man looked up from a large oak desk that was set in front of a window. The man behind the desk only had to turn to look out at his ranch.

He was in his sixties, with white hair and mustache that were well cared for. As he stood, Roxy noticed he was straight, tall and handsome, despite his age.

"Dave," the man said, "what's—oh, Sheriff. Nice to see you."

He came around the desk and shook the sheriff's hand.

"Mr. Newport, this is Roxy Doyle."

"Miss Doyle," the man greeted. "Please, both of you sit and tell me what I can do for you. Oh, I'm sorry. Coffee?"

"No, thanks," Evers said.

"Not for me, thanks," Roxy said.

"Then what can I do for you?"

"Yesterday three of your hands tried to kill Miss Doyle," the sheriff said.

"What—" Jesse started, but his boss waved him off.

"Who are we talkin' about?" Newport asked.

"Foster, Egan," the sheriff said, "and James."

Newport looked at his foreman.

"All three went missin' this mornin', boss."

"Where are they?" Newport asked.

"Foster and Egan are with the undertaker," Evers said, "James is still missin'."

"You killed them?" Newport asked.

"No," Evers said, "Miss Doyle did."

"She did, did she?" Newport said.

"They tried to bushwhack me outside on the street," she said. "I killed Foster and Egan, but the man named James ran away."

"I have a fourth man, Conroy, in a cell," Evers said. "Is he yours?"

"No," Dave Jesse said, "we have no one by that name."

"So you're here to tell me two of my men are dead," Newport said, "or are there more?"

"We wanted to know if James had returned to the ranch," Evers said. "And a first name would help."

"His full name is Martin James," Jesse said, "and he's not here."

"I could take a look around," the sheriff said.

"No, you can't," Newport said. "You'll have to take my word for it. He's not here. And if he does show up, he's fired." He looked at his foreman. "Got it?"

"I got it, sir."

Newport looked at Roxy and the sheriff.

"I don't employ law breakers," he said. "That'll have to be good enough for you."

The lawman looked at Roxy.

"I suppose it will," Evers said.

"Then Dave will see you out," Newport said. "I'm sorry this happened to you, Miss Doyle."

"So am I," she said.

On the way to the door Dave Jesse asked, "Why did they do it?"

"They thought I was somebody else," she said.

"I find that hard to believe," Jesse said.

***

Riding back to town Roxy asked Evers "So what did you think?"

"I've never had any reason to think Mr. Newport was breakin' the law."

"One of them was lying," Roxy said.

"And what makes you think that?" Evers asked.

"Because any time there's three men in the same room," she said, "at least one of them is lying."

"You think I'm lyin'?" he asked.

"No," she said, "but one of them was."

"Which one?"

"If I had to guess," she said, "Newport."

"Why him?"

"Did you notice," she asked, "he never asked why those men tried to kill me."

"But Dave Jesse did," he replied. "He could've been askin' for Newport."

"No," she said, "it was his own curiosity."

"Well," Evers said, "we'll know more if and when we catch Martin James."

Chapter Five

This time Roxy enjoyed the steak, then decided on one beer before turning in. Her intention was to leave town early the next day, rather than stay around and wait for someone else to make a try at her. If it happened again on the trail, or in another town, she would be ready for it. Not that she wasn't always ready for someone to take a shot at her. That was Clint Adams' rule one: always be ready.

She walked to the Timberlake Saloon, approaching the bar with all eyes on her. There was a time she thought about cutting her red hair off, and dressing in baggy clothes to hide her curves, so she could go unnoticed when she stopped in saloons. But in the end, she decided to always be herself and deal with whatever came along.

At the bar she said, "Beer."

"Comin' up, little lady," the grey-haired bartender said. He drew a mug of beer and set it in front of her.

"On the house," he said.

"Why?"

"First one, right?"

"Right. Thanks."

"Besides," he said, "you gunned down a couple of yahoos."

"That's worth a beer?"

"We don't like bushwhackers around here."

"You hear anyone else talking about bushwhacking?" she asked.

"Naw," he said. "This is usually a nice town."

"Yeah" she said, "I'm sure."

"Besides," he said, "those fellas was from the Bar-V, not from town. Maybe Newport will keep his men on the ranch from now on."

"You don't like Mr. Newport?" she asked.

The bartender looked around, but the place wasn't crowded and there was no one near enough to hear.

"I don't like rich ranchers," he said. "Too uppity."

"I know what you mean," she said.

"You want another, lemme know."

"Sure."

"But you'll hafta pay."

"Of course."

She was finishing her drink when the sheriff came through the batwing doors. He spotted her and walked over.

"Can I buy you a beer?" she asked him.

"I'm makin' my rounds," he said. "I didn't think you'd be out and about."

"One beer, and then I'm turning in," she said.

"And when are you leavin' town?"

"Tomorrow," she said. "Soon enough for you?"

"I just don't want any more trouble," he said.

"That makes two of us."

He looked around.

"Well," he said, "it's quiet here. Good-night."

" 'night."

As he turned to walk away, she said, "Sheriff, what was that name, again? The gal those bushwhackers mistook me for?"

"Archer, Liz Archer."

"Right, right," she said. "I'll remember that."

"Some folks call her Angel Eyes," he said, and left.

'Angel Eyes' sounded familiar to her. And now that she thought about it, so did Archer.

"Another?" the bartender said.

"No," she said, "one's enough. Thanks."

She turned and all eyes followed her once again as she left the saloon.

***

Roxy saddled her horse the next morning and walked it out of the livery. She found Sheriff Evers waiting there for her.

21

"Wanted to make sure I was leaving?" she asked.

"No hard feelin's," the lawman said, "but I don't want no more dead bodies on our streets."

"Neither do I," she said. "Especially mine."

She mounted up.

"Thanks for seeing me off, Sheriff," she said. "I won't be back."

"Suits me," he said.

Roxy turned her horse and rode out of town. Rather than leaving trouble behind, she was sure she would find some ahead of her, eventually.

Chapter Six

A week later Liz Archer, otherwise known as Angel Eyes, rode into the town of Grizzly Creek, Colorado. She had no business there. She was just drifting. She hadn't been in a town for two days, so she was looking forward to a hot meal, and a soft bed. She spotted the Grizzly House Hotel and reined in her horse in front of it.

She dismounted and started to go in, but from behind her a voice said, "Don't bother."

She turned and saw three men standing in the street, facing her.

"Are you talking to me?" she asked.

"You're Liz Archer, right?" one man asked. "Angel Eyes?"

"I've been called that."

"Then you won't be needing a room."

"And why not?"

"Because you'll be dead."

All three men went for their guns.

Liz had been taught by Clint Adams never to try fanning her gun. She was also taught *how* to fan the gun, if the need ever arose. The important thing was to keep a downward pressure on the barrel while fanning the hammer, so that you didn't jerk the barrel up, spoiling your aim.

Actually, there was no aim involved. You just had to make sure the barrel was pointed in the direction you were shooting.

She fanned the gun five times, firing the shots so close together that no one could have counted them. The three men jerked in the street, their guns dropping from their hands, and then fell to the dirt. Liz kept one live round in the gun, in case there was another shooter somewhere. When it was clear there was not, she ejected the spent shells and fed five live rounds back in. By the time she finished, there were two men wearing badges running toward them, and a small crowd gathering.

"Ma'am, you wanna just stand where you are?" the older man said.

"No problem," she said.

"I'm Sheriff Hal Charles. This is my deputy, Kevin Hove."

The younger man stood staring at her, transfixed by her beauty. He had never seen such a combination of blonde hair and blue eyes before.

"Kevin!" the sheriff snapped.

"Huh?"

"Check the bodies."

"Yessir."

Hove leaned over the three men, then stood and said, "They're all dead, Sheriff."

The sheriff looked around at the crowd.

"See if anyone here knows who they are," he said, then looked at Archer and asked, "Unless you know?"

"Not a clue," she said. "I just got to town, dismounted, and they braced me."

"Go!" he said to Hove.

"Yessir."

"So you never saw any of these men before?" the sheriff asked.

"Never."

"What reason would they have to kill you?"

"I don't know. I'm going to holster my gun, Sheriff."

"Good idea."

The sheriff walked to the three bodies and went through their pockets. He found a piece of paper in one man's pocket, took it out and unfolded it.

"Is this you?" he asked.

She looked at the paper and saw that it was a wanted poster with a woman's face drawn on it. It could have been her, but because it was only hand drawn, there was no way of knowing the hair or eye color.

"It could be me," she said.

Above the face it said, THIS WOMAN and below it $5,000 DEAD!

There was smaller print along the bottom, but the sheriff withdrew it before she could read it.

"Angel Eyes," he said. "Is that you?"

"I've been called that, yes," she said.

"Somebody wants you pretty bad," he said, "and dead, no question of dead or alive."

"Looks that way," she said. "I've had men like this try for me before, looking for a reputation. But this is a very deliberate act, done for money."

"You know anybody rich enough whose path you've crossed, who could post this . . . reward?"

"I'm afraid I don't."

The deputy returned and resumed staring at Archer.

"No one knows them, Sheriff. Seems they're strangers."

"Well, get some of these men to carry the bodies to the undertaker's."

"Yessir."

"Miss Archer, I'd like you to come to my office where we can discuss this further."

"I was just about to get myself a hotel room, Sheriff," she said. "And after that board my horse and get a meal. Can I come over to your office after that?"

"I don't see why not," he said. "Try Angie's, across the street. She does a good beef stew."

"Thank you," she said, "I'll see you right after I try it."

He turned and walked away as she entered the hotel lobby.

Chapter Seven

When Liz Archer entered the sheriff's office the man looked up from his desk. She hadn't noticed that afternoon how heavily lined his face was. It made gauging his age difficult. He could have been forty or sixty.

"How was the stew?" he asked.

"Like you said," she replied. "It was very good."

"Have a seat," he said. "I can offer you a cup of bad coffee."

"I'm used to bad coffee."

She sat and accepted the chipped mug from him.

"What do you need from me, Sheriff?" she asked.

"Actually not a thing," he said. "Turns out there were a few witnesses who saw those three brace you as you dismounted. They were also real impressed by the way you handled them."

"I did what I had to do," Archer said.

"I guess so," the sheriff said. "This must happen to you pretty often."

"Sometimes," Archer said. "But not for money."

"And you still have no idea who put this price out on you?"

"I've been thinking about it," she said. "There might be one or two people who want me dead, but I don't think they'd go this far. I think they'd want to pull the trigger themselves."

"Well," the lawman said, "I can't see any reason I need to keep you here. You could ride out in the mornin'."

"Are you telling me to get out of town?" she asked.

"I'm tellin' you that you can get out of town if you want," he said. "I got no reason to stop you."

"I could hang around long enough to find out who put that price on my head," she said. "But I have the feeling whoever did it's not local. So there's no point in me staying." She stood up. "I'll ride out in the morning."

"Good," the sheriff said, "but that price is gonna follow you wherever you go, so be careful."

"I start every day being careful," Archer told the lawman, "and go from there."

"Do me a favor," the sheriff said, "try not to kill anybody else between tonight and when you leave tomorrow."

"Like you said," she replied, "that price is still on my head. If I kill anyone else . . . well, that's going to be up to them."

"You could try just stayin' in your room."

"You're right, sheriff," she said, on her way to the door, "I could try that."

***

Liz Archer knew a man in Arizona and a man in Kansas who might want her dead. She had killed one's brother, and the other's son. Both events had taken place a few years ago. At that time, neither man had five thousand dollars to put on her head. Of course, since then one of them might have managed to come up with that much money.

She was nearer to Arizona, so it might be a good idea to go there and check. The sheriff was right, that price was going to follow her wherever she went. The next time somebody tried to collect, she was going to have to try and take them alive. Somebody looking to cash in must have some idea who was paying the freight.

She had respect for anyone who faced her fair-and-square on the street. But no respect for anyone *paying* to have her killed. Anybody using their money to get at her was a coward. That was the other reason she didn't really think those men from Arizona and Kansas were behind the reward. She wouldn't have called either of these people a coward.

Originally, she had intended to visit a saloon for a couple of beers, but then she decided, why tempt fate, and instead went to her hotel.

Chapter Eight

Roxy followed a rumor about her father to Texas. The town was called Tempest, and she heard that her father, bounty hunter Gavin Doyle, had tracked a man there. Since that might have been the last place anyone had seen him, that was where she headed.

As she rode into Tempest, she figured it was small enough for someone to remember her father. She decided to start with the local law.

"Holy Jesus!" the sheriff said when she entered his office. He was in his forties, with a heavy, black mustache and brown eyes that went wide when he saw her. "You're Lady Gunsmith."

"My name's Roxy Doyle," she said. "I assume you're the sheriff."

"Stan Simmons is my name," the lawman said. "Uh, what can I do for you, Miss Doyle?"

"I'm looking for someone," she said. "Gavin Doyle."

"The bounty hunter?"

"That's right," Roxy said. "I heard he was tracking somebody here."

"If he was, I didn't hear about it."

"So he didn't come in to claim a bounty, here?"

"No," he said. "Sorry. I guess you heard wrong."

"It's not the first time," she said.

"Wait, Doyle?" the sheriff said. "Is he—"

"—my father," she said. "I've been looking for him a long time."

"Then I'm really sorry for you," the lawman said.

"Yeah, thanks."

"You, uh, gonna stay in town?"

"Long enough to get a good night's sleep," she said. "Then I'll move on."

"Well," he said, "if I can do anythin' for ya while you're here, lemme know."

"That's nice of you, thanks," she said. "What hotel's got a decent mattress?"

"There's only two, but you want the Lexington, across the street. Livery stable's at the end of the street."

"Thanks," she said, again, and left the office.

She walked her horse to the stable, got it boarded, then carried her rifle and saddlebags to the hotel.

The young desk clerk gaped at her as she approached the desk.

"Can I get a room?" she asked.

"Huh? Oh, sure." He turned the register book her way. "Sign in."

She did and was handed a key for room nine.

"I hope this room doesn't overlook the front street," she said

"No, Ma'am."

"Good."

She went upstairs, stowed her gear and came back down. It was the same in every town. Board your horse, get a room, then a meal. But in between such stops were days on the trail, sleeping on the ground and eating beans, so these stops were welcome, whether she found her father or not.

"Where can I get a good meal?" she asked the clerk.

"A small café down the street called Muffins," the clerk said.

"Do they make good muffins?"

"Among other things," he told her, then laughed. "It's only a name."

"I'll try it."

Roxy left the hotel and walked down the street to Muffins. It was a small storefront with the name stenciled on the window, but the inside was much larger, to her surprise.

"A table?" a waiter asked.

"In the back, please."

"Certainly."

Since the place was not yet half full, getting a table she wanted was not a problem.

"What can I serve you?" the waiter asked.

"Do you have a special of the day?"

"We do."

"I'll have it."

"Do you want to know what it is?"

"Surprise me."

"Yes, Ma'am."

"Meanwhile I'll have coffee, strong and black."

"Yes, Ma'am."

She drank her coffee and studied the other diners in the room. Men eating alone, a young couple more interested in each other than their food, families with one or two small children, an older woman alone. A few of the men were stealing looks at her, but it was an older woman who stared brazenly. Roxy smiled at her and nodded, but the woman's expression didn't change—in fact, there was none.

The waiter brought a plate and set it down. Thankfully, it wasn't fish.

"What is it?" she asked.

"Pork sausage with sauerkraut."

"What's sour-kraut?" she asked.

"Thinly sliced cabbage, salt. And a secret ingredient."

"What ingredient?"

"It's a secret," he said.

She tasted it.

"It's good," she said.

"Enjoy."

She sliced a piece of sausage and tried it with the sauerkraut.

Even better.

Starving, she ate voraciously.

Chapter Nine

Roxy was finishing her last bite when she saw people running past the window. The waiter went to the door and stepped out for a moment, then came back in. Roxy called him over.

"What's going on?" she asked.

"Seems like there's gonna be a gunfight," he said. "Five against one."

"Those are not good odds," she said. "Who's the one?"

"I'm not sure," he said. "Somebody said it was a blonde woman."

Roxy stood up.

"Where's this happening?"

"Down the street." He pointed.

Roxy paid her bill and hurried out to the street. She headed toward the rest of the crowd. pushing her way through a mass of people who were apparently looking on. When she got to the front, she saw five men standing in the street facing a blonde woman in front of a hotel.

***

Liz Archer had arrived in Tempest the previous evening. She'd had breakfast in her hotel, and then went back to her room for a rest. She was in town after a three day ride and needed the rest.

As it became late afternoon, she decided to go out and get a bite to eat. When she stepped from the hotel, she saw the five men standing in the street.

"That's far enough, Miss Angel Eyes," the man in the center said.

"Somethin' I can do for you boys?" she asked.

"There's a price on your head, Miss Angel Eyes," the man said. "We intend to collect."

Archer saw the crowd gathering off to her left, obviously interested in watching.

"What makes you think I'm Angel Eyes?" she asked.

"You fit the description," the man said. "Blonde hair, that gun on your hip, right down to the orange bandana around your neck. Oh, it's you, all right."

"Okay, it's me," she said. "Now what?"

"We trailed you here, and now we cash in," he said. "You're wanted, dead."

Archer noticed the red-haired woman push her way to the front of the crowd. She was wearing a gun on her right hip, and if she was who Archer thought she was, she knew how to use it.

Was she going to have to face Lady Gunsmith, too?

***

Roxy saw that the action was about to take place in front of her hotel. She couldn't hear what was being said, but she knew what was about to happen, she didn't approve of the odds. She strode into the street and stopped just behind the men.

"You boys don't seem to be playing fair," she said.

Three of the five men turned their heads. The middle man and one other kept their eyes locked on Liz Archer.

"Who is it?" the middle man asked.

"It's a woman, boss," one of the men said. "Long red hair, real pretty, wearin' a gun."

"Keep your eyes on the blonde," the middle man said. As the men did, he turned to look at Roxy. "Well, I'll be. What's Lady Gunsmith doin' here? Collectin' the reward? Sorry. But we saw her first."

"I'm not here for any reward," Roxy said. "Five to one odds goes against the grain for me."

"So you want me to face her alone?" the man asked. "You think I'm crazy?"

"You may be," Roxy said, "but that wasn't what I had in mind."

"Oh?"

"I thought I'd change the odds a bit."

"How?"

39

Roxy shrugged.

"Five-to-two seems a bit more fair."

"Why would you stand with her?" he asked.

"I told you," Roxy said, "I don't like odds like this. So I can do it from behind you, or I can stand by her side. I'll leave the set-up to you."

"Behind us wouldn't be fair," he complained.

"Oh, so now you're worried about bein' fair?" Liz Archer asked, speaking up for the first time since Roxy's arrival on the scene.

"We'll see," Roxy said, and started to circle the men, keeping a sharp eye on them.

She made it all the way to Liz Archer's side.

"Hope you don't mind me buttin' in," Roxy said in a low tone.

"I don't know why you'd want to butt in," Liz Archer said. "But the more the merrier."

"I'm in," Roxy said.

The two women faced the five men, who were looking around at each other.

The man in the center laughed. "There's only two of 'em and they're women. We're lookin' at five thousand dollars. So get ready."

"Do we wait for them to get ready?" Archer asked.

"Hell, no," Roxy said, and both women drew their guns and began firing.

Chapter Ten

A gasp went through the crowd as the women fired and the men in the street danced and fell as lead hit them.

"Okay, ladies," a voice said from their right, "put your guns up."

Both women turned and found themselves facing the sheriff. He had both of his hands out, and they were empty.

"Easy!" the lawman said. "It's over. Holster those guns."

"Sorry, Sheriff," Roxy said, "but we've got to check and see if they're all dead before we put our guns away."

"Stay where you are," he said. "I'll check 'em."

They watched as he went to each fallen man and bent over them, then stood and turned.

"They're all dead," he said. "Now could you put your guns away?"

They each ejected the spent shells, reloaded, then holstered their weapons.

"Now why don't you hit the saloon for a drink, and then come to my office?" he said.

"Are we in trouble?" Liz Archer asked.

"There were a lot of witnesses," the sheriff said. "I'm gonna talk to them all. Just come to my office in a couple of hours."

"Right," Archer said, then looked at Roxy. "Buy you a drink?"

"I thought you'd never ask."

As they left the scene, the sheriff was yelling, "I need some men to take these bodies off the street!"

***

Roxy and Archer went to the nearest saloon, one called The Tributary Saloon. The tall, beautiful blonde and slightly shorter, but just as beautiful redhead attracted the attention of the dozen or so men who were present. They went to the bar, where the young bartender smiled at them.

"Ladies, what can I do for you?"

"Two beers," Archer said.

"Comin' up."

He went down the bar, and came back with two frosty mugs.

"What was all that shootin' about?" he asked, as he set them down.

"Five men picked on the wrong woman," Roxy said.

Roxy Doyle Meets an Angel

"Women," Archer corrected. "It was five against two."

"Five?" the bartender said. "Damn! You two killed five men?"

"They didn't leave us much choice," Archer said.

"How much?" Roxy asked. "For the beers."

"Let's say these are on the house."

"Why?" Archer asked, suspiciously.

"You're celebratin', right?"

"I don't celebrate killing men," Roxy said.

"Me, neither."

"Then celebrate bein' alive."

Roxy and Archer looked at each other, then Roxy said, "Sounds good."

They picked up the beer and drank half, then put the mugs down and looked around.

"Quiet place you've got here," Archer said.

"Come back after dark," he said. "There'll be a big difference."

"Maybe we will," Roxy said.

"Well," the bartender said, "finish your beers, lemme know if you want another. I got other customers."

Two men had walked in and taken up space at the far end of the bar. They took sidelong glances at the two beautiful women. Both men were in their thirties, and pleasant looking. Roxy didn't anticipate any trouble from them. But she had other ideas . . .

"What do you think of those two?" she asked Archer.

Archer glanced over.

"They don't look like trouble. They're not even wearing guns."

"Yeah," Roxy said, "but they look like fun."

"Have you got time for fun?" Archer asked.

"I like to let loose sometimes," Roxy said. "What do you say?"

Archer called out, "Bartender!"

He came over.

"Ready for another?"

"We are," Archer said, "and we wanna buy those two men a beer."

"If you say so, Ma'am."

"Is that a bad idea?" Roxy asked.

"Not at all," the barman said

"Do you know them?" Roxy asked.

"They're a couple of hands from the AZ ranch."

"What are they like?" Archer asked.

"They're a couple of good boys," the bartender said.

"Well then, give 'em their beers and ask 'em if they'll sit with us," Roxy said.

"I'm sure they'll be glad to oblige you," the bartender said.

44

Chapter Eleven

Roxy, Archer and the ranch hands took a table in the back and started to get acquainted. As it got later, the place began to fill up. Many of the men were there when Roxy and Archer outgunned the five men, so they kept their distance.

The ranch hands were Ray and Paul. They took turns going to buy drinks. When Paul came back to the table he leaned over and said something in Ray's ear.

"What's goin' on?" Archer asked. "Secrets?"

The two men looked at her, then Paul spoke.

"Fella at the bar told us what happened before," he said. "He said you girls gunned down five men between you."

"Is that true?" Ray asked.

"It's true," Roxy said. "They didn't give us much choice."

"Does that scare ya?" Archer asked.

"I wish I'd been there ta see it, is all," Ray said.

"So you find it excitin'?" she asked. "A woman with a gun, I mean?"

"Real excitin'," Paul said.

"Me, too," Ray added.

It seemed to have developed that Ray was paying attention to Liz Archer, while Paul was eyeing Roxy. The women didn't particularly care which way they were going to go. These two young men were earmarked for a single night of fun and frolic, nothing more.

"Do you boys have to get back to your ranch tonight?" Roxy asked.

"Not really," Paul said. "Why, what did you have in mind?"

"We're at the hotel across the street," Archer said.

"You each have your own room?" Ray asked.

"We do," Archer said.

"We didn't even know each other when we checked in and discovered later we were in the same hotel."

"Well," Ray said, "I ain't never been in the hotel. I'd kinda like to see a room there."

"Me, too," Paul said, though by the way he was looking at Liz Archer it was clear what he actually wanted to see.

"Well," Roxy said, "let's go."

But as the four stood to leave the saloon, Sheriff Simmons entered and started for them.

"You ladies in trouble with the law?" Ray asked.

"I hope not," Roxy said.

"Let's see," Archer said.

"Ladies," Simmons said, "a moment of your time, please?"

"Can we buy you a drink, Sheriff?"

"No, that's okay," he said, then looked at the two cowhands. "You boys mind waitin' at the bar? This won't take long."

"Whatever you say, Sheriff," Ray said, and they both drifted away.

"Have a seat," he said, and they all sat.

"What's on your mind, Sheriff."

"You two," Simmons said. "I want you to leave town tomorrow."

"Why's that?" Archer asked.

"I don't want any more killin' in my town."

"Neither do we," Roxy said.

"Yeah, but you might not have a choice," he said. "Like with those five."

Roxy looked at Archer.

"He's right," she said. "Somebody else is going to try for that price on your head, sooner or later."

"I can take care of myself," Archer said.

"I know that," Roxy said. She looked at the lawman. "Don't worry, Sheriff. I'll be gone in the morning."

"And you?" he asked Archer.

"Why not?" Archer said. "There's nothin' here for me."

"That's good," the lawman said, standing up. "Have a nice night."

"We intend to," Archer said.

Roxy and Archer stood and walked to the bar, where Ray and Paul were standing.

"Everythin' all right?" Paul asked.

"Just fine," Roxy said.

"You boys ready?" Archer said.

"We been ready," Ray said.

Archer linked her arm in Ray's and Roxy did the same to Paul. They walked out of the saloon together and crossed the street to the hotel. When they passed the desk clerk on the way to the stairs, he smiled. Roxy had considered the clerk for some fun if she didn't find anyone else, but he was too young.

They went up the stairs and down the hall. Archer's room came first. She unlocked the door and allowed Ray to walk in ahead of her.

"Have a good night," she said to Roxy.

"You, too, Liz."

Archer went in and closed the door. Roxy and Paul walked to her door. He waited for her to unlock it, then said, "After you."

"Oh, a gentleman."

Roxy entered the room. Paul came in after her and closed the door. Then she turned and walked into his arms.

Chapter Twelve

Roxy was disappointed.

Paul was young and fit, but be didn't seem to know what to do with a woman if she wasn't a whore. She paid attention to his body, running her mouth over him until she reached his swollen cock. But when she took him into her mouth, he went tense and she knew he was about to explode, so she released him, wrapped her hand around the base of his penis and squeezed. That seemed to hold the eruption back. Then she mounted him, took his cock inside, and just rode him until he finished with a loud roar.

"Wow," he said, breathlessly, "that was amazin'."

"Yeah," she said, sliding off him. "You can let yourself out. I've got to get some sleep. The sheriff wants me out of town early."

"Huh?" Paul asked, confused. "I thought we'd, you know, do it again after an hour or so."

"Sorry, lover," she said. "Can't do it. You tired me out."

"Yeah, well," he said in a depressed tone, "okay."

He got up, dressed, seemed unsure about trying to kiss her goodbye, but then just left.

Thoroughly unsatisfied with the time she spent with him, she drifted off to sleep.

***

In the room next door Liz Archer was having a little more luck with Ray who—while he didn't seem to know much about women—was willing to learn. She guided him as to what to do, and when she pushed his face down between her legs, he went to work with his tongue willingly.

When she pushed him away and flipped him over, he very happily gave himself up to her, as she licked her way down to his cock and took it into her mouth. While his penis seemed to swell even more as she sucked, he managed to keep himself from finishing in her mouth too soon. When she felt he'd had enough, though, she released him, moved onto her back next to him and said, "Come on, cowboy!"

"Yes, Ma'am," he gushed.

Anxiously, he positioned himself between her legs, gazing for a moment at the golden triangle of hair that was there, moist and glistening, and then drove his hard cock into her. She was glad he wasn't gentle because she needed the energy now.

51

She wondered idly if Roxy was having as much fun with Paul, then stopped thinking and just started feeling . . .

***

When Roxy woke the following morning, she was still feeling frustrated and dissatisfied by her session with the cowhand, Paul. Maybe the young desk clerk would have been trainable. She hoped Liz had a better time with her ranch hand.

***

Archer woke with her legs tangled with Ray's. She kicked until he woke up, and then said, "Time for you to go."

He mumbled something, but she used both of her feet to push him off the bed. He hit the floor with a thud, then looked up at her.

"I mean it," she said. "Time to go."

"Okay, okay," Ray said, getting to his feet. He pulled on his clothes, then turned and looked at her, lying there naked in the bed. She could see him getting excited again.

"No more!" she said. "I have to get ready to leave town. Go!"

He moved to the door, looking like a kicked dog, and left.

She rubbed her face with her hands, then reached down to rub her crotch.

"Jesus!" she said.

The night's exertions should be enough to hold her for a while.

***

Roxy was waiting in the lobby when she saw Paul scurry by. Apparently, Archer did have a better time last night than she had. She decided to remain there and wait for Archer to come down.

When the blonde appeared, she looked tired.

"I thought we'd have breakfast together," Roxy said, "before we leave town."

"Sounds good to me."

They went into the dining room, sat at a back table and ordered.

"I saw your cowhand leave," Roxy said. "Seems yours was better than mine."

"He was young and anxious," Archer said, "and, if I had more time, trainable. Yours?"

"I kicked him out last night," she said. "He got his, and he was done."

"Sorry to hear that," Archer said.

They both had a cup of coffee while they waited for their eggs.

"Where are you headed after this?" Archer asked.

"Nowhere in particular," Roxy said. She had told Archer about her search for her father, while they sat in the saloon. "I don't have any more rumored sighting to follow at the moment. What about you?"

"I'm not headin' anywhere in particular. But wherever I go, I'll still have this price on my head."

"And while I'm being mistaken for you," Roxy pointed out, "so will I.

"I don't understand that," Archer said. "You've got all that gorgeous red hair. It's sad some men can't see the difference."

"They see a gal wearing a gun in a holster," Roxy said. "That's all."

"I tell you what," Archer said. "Why don't we ride together for a while. We can watch each other's backs and, if it happens again, maybe we can take the next one alive and see what he knows."

"That sounds okay to me," Roxy said. "I'll be glad for the company."

At that point the waiter came with their breakfast, and they began to eat.

Chapter Thirteen

After breakfast they carried their saddlebags and rifles to the livery to pick up their horses. Roxy saw that Archer was riding a bay mare. She herself had a sorrel, these days. She changed horses often and didn't name any of them. She knew she wouldn't have them long enough to become attached.

They walked their animals outside, where they found Sheriff Simmons waiting.

"Wanted to see us off?" Roxy asked.

"Just makin' sure," he said.

"Don't worry," Archer said, putting her foot in her stirrup, "we're goin'."

"No offense meant, ladies," he said, with a shrug. "Just doin' my job."

"No offense taken, Sheriff," Roxy said, mounting up.

The lawman watched as the women rode out of his town. With a sigh of relief, he turned and walked back to his office.

***

They rode for most of the day without speaking, just enjoying the feel of their horses beneath them and the miles going by. As dusk began to fall, they made camp and whipped up a plate of beans.

"I don't mind eatin' this way for a night or two," Archer said.

"Makes a steak taste that much better when you do get one," Roxy pointed out.

"You know," Archer said, "we're gonna have to pick a town to stop in."

They had bypassed several during the day, wondering if they would run into more bounty hunters. Even if the price on Archer's head wasn't legitimate, bounty hunters were sure to know about it. Roxy wondered if her father would try for it. That would be an odd coincidence, and Clint Adams had tried to convince Roxy that there was no such thing as coincidence.

"We might as well keep passing up the small ones and pick a good-sized town," Roxy said.

"There's bound to be somebody there lookin' to cash in on me," Archer said. "I wonder if the bounty's been put out, only in Texas?"

"We'd have to leave Texas to find that out," Roxy pointed out.

"We can do that," Archer said, "unless you object."

"Don't make no difference to me," Roxy said. "The way we're headed, we'll be hitting New Mexico in a week or so."

"Suits me," Archer said. "But maybe we'll clear this up by then."

"Only if we can take somebody alive," Roxy said. "Trouble is, it's hard not to kill somebody who's trying to kill you," she pointed out.

"That's true," Archer said. "There's no time for trick shootin' when somebody's slingin' lead your way."

Roxy put down her empty plate and coffee cup.

"I'll clean those and put 'em away."

"I'll check the horses before we turn in," Archer said.

They each saw to their chosen chore, then spread their bedrolls and prepared to turn in.

After a few moments Roxy asked, "You awake?"

"Yeah."

"I was thinking."

"Me, too."

They propped themselves up on an elbow and looked at each other.

"I'll take the first watch," Roxy said.

Archer laid back down.

"Wake me in four hours."

Roxy nodded and went to the fire while Archer fell asleep.

***

The way Archer came instantly awake when Roxy shook her impressed Roxy. She knew when Archer returned the favor in the morning, she would be anything but alert. But Archer seemed to sense that and woke Roxy with a cup of hot coffee in her hand.

"Thanks," Roxy said, accepting it gratefully.

"Got some bacon in the pan when you're ready," Archer said.

"I'm ready now," Roxy said, getting to her feet.

She staggered to the fire and accepted a plate of crisp bacon from Archer.

"I was thinkin' about Amarillo," Archer said, while they ate.

"What about it?"

"As the next place to stop," Archer said. "And it's about a hundred miles from the New Mexico border.

"You've given this a lot of thought," Roxy said.

"More than you think," Archer said. "Once we hit New Mexico I was thinkin' our next stop could be Tucumcari."

"What's in Tucumcari?" Roxy asked.

"It's the first town we'll come to in New Mexico," Archer replied. "Not that big, but pretty busy."

"You've been there before," Roxy observed.

"A time or two," Archer said.

"All right, then," Roxy said, "Amarillo, and then Tucumcari. Agreed."

Chapter Fourteen

Amarillo was a bustling town, with businessmen and cattle barons making use of the stockyards and railroads. No one paid special attention to the women riding in, no matter how beautiful they were.

"I like not being stared at," Archer said.

"So do I," Roxy said. "Let's find a hotel."

"It's Amarillo," Archer said, "There's a lot of 'em."

They stopped at one called The Amarillo House and stared at it.

"Looks expensive," Roxy said. "How are you fixed?"

"Pretty good, for a change," Archer said. "I just did a job that paid well. What about you?"

"Same here," Roxy said. "Come on, let's get a couple of rooms."

They dismounted and went inside. On the way in a man bulled his way out coming between the women and knocking them off balance.

"Get outta my way!" he grumbled, drunkenly. "Hotel thinks it's too good for the likes of me."

He staggered off, and they went inside, shaking their heads. At the front desk a middle-aged clerk wearing a dark suit smiled at them.

"I'm sorry about that, ladies," he said. "We don't allow drunks to check into the Amarillo House."

"That's nice to hear," Roxy said. "We'd like a couple of rooms."

"Sorry, but we've only got one room left. It's got two beds, though. You want it? You probably won't find another one without goin' further into the city."

Roxy and Archer looked at each other, and then Roxy said, "We'll take it."

"Then sign in, please," he said, reversing the directory.

"What's goin' on in town that rooms are scarce?" Archer asked.

"Place is bulging with cattlemen," the clerk said. "I'm afraid it might be kinda loud in some of the rooms."

"I thought you didn't give rooms to drunks?" Roxy said. "Doesn't that go for drunken cowboys?"

"Well, they weren't drunk when they checked in," he said. "After that, who knows? And in some of the rooms there's three or four of them. Still want the room?"

"Yes, we do," Roxy said, signing in after Archer.

"Any luggage?" he asked.

"Just saddlebags," Archer said. "We can handle them ourselves?"

"Do you have a stable?" Roxy asked.

"Yes, ma'am. I'll have your horses taken care of. Any idea how long you'll be staying?"

"Might be one night," Roxy said, "maybe two."

"Depends on how good the food is in your dining room," Archer added.

The man smiled and said, "Well, in that case you might be here a week."

"We'll see," Roxy said.

They went out and got their saddlebags and rifles from their horses, then turned the animals over to the man from the hotel's stable.

When they got to their rooms, they found it was big enough for the two of them, with two beds, four feet apart.

"This'll do," Roxy said, tossing her saddlebags on one of them.

"Why'd you pick that one?" Archer asked. "It's nearer the window."

Roxy grinned and said, "It was an easier toss."

"Well, it suits me," Archer said, dropping her saddlebags on the other bed. "Wanna get a meal?"

"You bet," Roxy said. "I want to see if the clerk was bragging or telling the truth. But I think we better wash up first."

There was a sink with running water and a mirror over it.

"I'll go first," Archer said, and unbuttoned her shirt. She took it off, revealing herself to be naked beneath it. She had creamy white skin, full breasts with pink nipples. Roxy found herself staring at the girl's beautiful body, then looked away.

"You don't have to close your eyes," Archer said, "I'm not shy."

She ran the water and used a bar of soap and a cloth to clean her breasts, arms, hands and armpits before grabbing a towel.

"Your turn," she said to Roxy, facing her, still naked to the waist. She put her hands on her hips and asked, "Do you want me to leave?"

"It's not necessary," Roxy said. She undid her shirt and took it off. She was also naked underneath, as there was no need for frilly underthings on the trail.

While she was shorter than Archer, she was as buxom, with full breasts with heavy undersides, and copper-colored nipples. She soaped herself, noticing that her nipples were getting hard. That usually only happened when she was sexually aroused. In the mirror she could see Archer, still standing with her breasts exposed, looking her over from behind. She wondered if Angel Eyes was one of those women who also liked other women. Roxy had never had such an experience.

They each took a clean shirt from their saddlebags and put them on, watching each other do every button.

"You have a beautiful body," Archer said.

"So do you," Roxy said.

"Well," Archer said, tying an orange bandana around her neck, "we better feed them so we can keep 'em beautiful."

They went down to the crowded lobby and walked across for the entrance of the dining room. It, too, seemed fairly crowded, but they spotted a few empty tables.

"Ladies," an older, white-haired man in a tuxedo greeted them.

"Can we get a table?" Roxy asked.

"Of course," he said.

"How about that one, in the back?" Roxy asked.

"Very well," the man said, "if you will follow me, please."

He led the way across the crowded dining room.

Chapter Fifteen

They both ordered a steak dinner, Roxy rare, Archer well done.

"I've never been able to eat well-done meat," Roxy said, observing the piece of beef on Archer's plate.

"I've tried it rare," Archer said. "I just prefer it this way."

As they started to eat, they noticed that they were finally drawing attention.

"Not as many distractions in here," Archer said, "so we're the center of attention."

"They're probably looking at you," Roxy said.

"You're a gorgeous woman, Roxy," Archer said. "Maybe they're lookin' at you."

"I mean," Roxy said, "because of the price on your head."

"Ah . . ."

They both looked around and half a dozen men quickly looked away.

"They all look like businessmen," Roxy said. "And I don't see guns."

"Then maybe," Archer said, "they just like pretty girls."

"That might be it," Roxy agreed, "but we'd better stay alert, anyway."

"What do you intend to do after this?" Archer asked.

"I thought I'd walk around a bit, take a look at Amarillo," Roxy replied.

"I tell you what," Archer said. "Why don't I walk around, and you trail along behind me. If somebody tries for the price on my head, you'll grab 'em."

"Hopefully before they shoot you."

"Naturally."

"I think we can do that for a few hours," Roxy said. "Then we should stop in a saloon for a beer. I'd just as soon nobody steps up and tries."

"I don't know what would be ideal," Archer said. "I'd like to grab somebody and see what we can find out. If I knew who put that price on me, I could do somethin' about it."

"It would be nice to know that somebody's trying to kill you just because of your reputation."

"Just a normal day, hmm?"

"For the likes of us," Roxy said, "yes."

"Maybe if we stay together permanently," Archer said, "nobody would try."

"Or we'd get on each other's nerves," Roxy said. "I've never ridden with one person for very long."

"Neither have I," Archer said. "Maybe we should give it a try."

"First things first," Roxy said. "We can talk about that after we find out who wants you dead, probably for personal reasons."

"Agreed."

The waiter cleared their plates and brought them coffee and pie, cherry for Roxy, blueberry for Archer.

When they finished, they left the dining room, feeling many sets of eyes following their progress.

Outside, in front of the hotel, they paused and looked at the street.

"Where should we walk to?" Archer asked. "Or should we just stroll aimlessly?"

"Let's try heading for the stockyards," Roxy suggested.

"Interested in cows?" Archer asked,

"More like cowhands," Roxy said. "Don't forget, I didn't enjoy my last one as much as you did yours."

"All right, then," Archer said. "The stockyards it is."

There was a doorman in front of the hotel, who they had bypassed when they arrived. Archer decided to put him to use.

"Excuse me," she said, "but which way are the stockyards?"

"That way, Ma'am," the tall man said. "But why would a pretty woman like you want to go to a smelly place like that?"

"You know of a better place for a pretty woman to go?" she asked.

"I get off duty in two hours," he said. "I could show you around."

"Two hours, eh?" she said. "I might take you up on that."

Archer walked back to Roxy.

"Flirting with the doorman?" Roxy said.

"He's got some seasoning," Archer said. "And broad shoulders. I'll just keep him in mind. Meanwhile, the stockyards are that way."

"After you," Roxy said.

Archer went down the steps to the street and started walking in the direction of the stockyards.

***

The walk to the stockyards was uneventful. Roxy noticed men as they watched Archer walk by, but then again, those same men watched her. They were both attracting attention—admiring looks from men, dirty looks from women—so Roxy didn't think their plan was going to work.

When they reached the busy stockyards, they saw that not only was it filled with cattle and cattlemen, but there was a livestock auction in progress. Roxy joined Archer at the corral, and they both watched for a while, still keeping alert. But at this location, all the attention seemed to be on livestock.

Chapter Sixteen

"You know," Archer asked, as they watched, "I never asked you why your horse doesn't have a name?"

"I never keep a horse very long," Roxy said. "I don't want to get attached."

"That's funny," Archer said, "I feel the same way." She looked at Roxy. "We're findin' we have more and more in common."

"So we are."

Several horses went for a great deal of money, and Archer said, "I wonder why men love horses so much? I can think of so many other things to spend that much money on."

"Like what?"

Archer smiled.

"Like us."

They watched for a short time longer, then Roxy said, "Back to the hotel?"

"Why not?" Archer said. "I've seen enough of men spendin' money on horses."

They turned together and found themselves facing three men, all wearing guns in holsters.

"You," the man in the center said, "can go. We're here for her." He pointed at Archer.

"You want her," Roxy said, "you get me, too."

The three men exchanged glances.

"She's Lady Gunsmith, Hank," one of the others said. "I've seen her before."

"We're only supposed to hafta deal with Angel Eyes," the other man said. "I ain't goin' against both of 'em."

"Oh, but you are," Archer said. "Unless you tell us who sent you."

"Sent us?" the middle man asked.

"Who put the price on her head?" Roxy asked.

"How do we know?" one asked. "We saw her walking by and knew about the price, but we don't know who's behind it."

"Then how did you intend to collect?" Archer asked.

"Well . . ." one started.

"It's on the poster," the middle one said.

"Ah," Roxy said, "and where's the poster?"

The men looked at each other, again.

"Come on, come on," Roxy said, "either draw your guns, or hand over the poster."

"Give it to them, Hank, and let's get outta here," one of the men said.

Hank reached inside his shirt and brought a rolled-up poster out. He tossed it to the dirt.

"There!"

"Now git!" Archer said. "Before we change our minds."

The three men turned and ran. Roxy walked over and picked up the poster. When she turned to Archer she could see, behind her, that the men at the auction had paused to watch the action.

"Back to your auction, gents!" Roxy shouted. "Nothing to see here."

"Let's head back and look at this later," Archer suggested.

"Right," Roxy said, as they left the stockyards.

***

The three men didn't run far.

"Hold up!" Hank said.

"What for?" one of the other men, Les, asked. "That was a bust."

"I'm not givin' up yet," Hank said. "They can't stay together forever. We just have to watch 'em and wait for our chance."

Les looked at the third man, Kyle, who said, "Hank's got a point."

"Let's get off the street and wait for 'em to go by," Hank said. "Five thousand's too much to pass up."

The other two men agreed.

***

They started for the hotel, but instead decided to stop at a saloon. They had passed several along the way, and chose a small one called The Copper Penny Saloon.

It seemed half-full, so they had their pick of tables. They got two beers from a friendly bartender and sat in the back.

"Let's see it," Archer said.

Roxy unfurled the poster and put it on the table. They used their beer mugs to hold it flat. There was a drawing of Archer's face, and, in bold print, it said WANTED: DEAD ONLY. $5,000.

"Not a good likeness," Archer said.

There was a short description that said she was tall, blonde, and comely, wears an orange bandana.

"Comely?" Archer said, raising one eyebrow.

"Look at the bottom," Roxy said.

In small print it said: COLLECT FROM THE BANK OF MILLFORD, ARIZONA. BRING PROOF.

"Well," Roxy said, "this gives me an idea."

"Me, too," Archer said. "You're gonna collect the bounty, and here," she said, touching the bandana around her neck, "is the proof."

"Exactly what I was thinking."

"And since you're Lady Gunsmith," Archer said, "they won't question that you were able to outdraw me."

The two women eyed each other across the table, the same thought going through their minds.

Which of them actually *was* faster?

Chapter Seventeen

They finished their beer and, when armed with a second one each, discussed their next move.

"We could leave in the morning for Millford," Roxy said.

"But you'll have to ride in alone," Archer pointed out. "I'll make my way in after I've disguised myself."

"You'll have to do more than just tuck that blonde hair under your hat."

"I'll figure somethin' out along the way," Archer said. "Meanwhile, there's still those three men to consider."

"You don't think they're done?" Roxy asked.

"Do you?" Archer asked, "with five thousand dollars at stake?"

"No, I don't," Roxy said. "I think we can expect some sort of ambush before we leave Amarillo."

"We'll be extra alert," Archer said.

They finished their beer and left the small saloon, stopping just outside to check the street.

"What about you and your doorman?" Roxy asked.

"Yeah, well," Archer said, with a sly smile, "that'd be kind of hard. We're sharin' a room, remember?"

"I could make myself scarce."

"I'd rather we stay together," Archer said. "Safer that way."

"We'd better get back, then," Roxy said.

They stepped into the street and started back, keeping a sharp eye in all directions.

***

"You wanna take 'em now?" Les asked Hank.

They watched from an alley as the two women started walking in the direction of their hotel.

"No," Hank said, "they'd be waitin' for it."

"Then when?" Kyle asked.

"They'll probably be headin' for Millford tomorrow," Hank said. "We got plenty of time between here and there to make our move. All we gotta do is bide our time. Meanwhile, we'll watch their hotel in shifts, just in case they decide to leave in the dead of night."

***

When they got back to the hotel, they found the doorman waiting out front.

"I'll let him down easy," Archer said.

Roxy stood to one side as the blonde went over and spoke to the man. He seemed disappointed when she turned and walked away.

"Okay," Archer said, "let's go."

"He does have broad shoulders," Roxy said.

"Roxy, no," Archer said, turning her friend around, "we're not gonna both take 'im to our room. We'll be up all night."

Roxy knew Archer was right, but she was still feeling some frustration over her last sexual encounter with the young cowhand. But she was just going to have to put up with it.

They walked through the busy lobby to the stairs and up to the second floor. The hotel had an elevator, but neither of them was willing to get into it. It was just too much of a newfangled thing.

In their room Archer said, "Okay, we had a meal, and a walk and a couple of beers. What's left?"

"We turn in for the night, get an early start after breakfast."

"You got a deck of cards?"

"No."

"Me, neither," Archer said, shaking her head.

Roxy knew Archer she was still thinking about the doorman with the broad shoulders.

"Then I guess we have no choice but to turn in," Archer said.

"Do you have any ideas about who might have posted this bounty, now that we know about Millford?"

"There's one man in Arizona I was thinkin' about," Archer said. "It might be him. But he doesn't live in Millford. I guess we'll find out when we get there."

Roxy undressed with her back to Archer. She was considering sleeping in her shirt, but when she turned she saw that Archer was getting into bed, naked, with nothing covering her. She saw Roxy looking at her.

"I hope you don't mind," the blonde said. "I don't like wearing anything to bed. I like feelin' free. Goodnight." She rolled over with her back to Roxy. "You can douse the light when you're ready."

Roxy stood for a moment, studying Archer's pale back and butt. She had really never given any thought to being with a woman before, but she had never met one as appealing as Liz Archer. She could almost feel the heat radiating from the woman's body, even across the room.

She decided to also get into bed naked, as it was the way she usually slept, anyway. But she pulled the sheet up to cover herself.

Chapter Eighteen

Roxy slept fitfully, fully aware of Liz Archer sleeping peacefully in the bed beside her. It seemed to her that Archer was the one who should be tossing and turning, since the price was on *her* head. But the blonde was breathing easily, not having moved a muscle since falling asleep.

While Roxy, as Lady Gunsmith, seemed to be better known than Liz Archer, as Angel Eyes, Archer was several years older and the more experienced of the two.

Roxy got out of bed and walked to the sink. She looked at herself in the mirror and frowned. Her hair was like a huge bird's nest, and she thought she looked haggard and dirty. There was a door next to the sink, which the day before she assumed was a closet. Now she opened it, and saw a bathtub. She wondered if she could take a bath without waking Archer. She decided to try.

Everything she needed was in the room. Cloths, towels, soap. She stepped in, closed the door behind her, and then tried the faucet to fill the tub. As the water came out it sounded uncomfortably loud to her. She cracked the door to look at Archer, who hadn't moved.

Once the tub was full, she realized it was cold water. She knew she could get somebody from the hotel staff to heat it for her, but she was satisfied that it was wet, and she would be able to get clean.

She gritted her teeth and, soap in hand, lowered herself into the water. As she got used to the cold water, she began to soap herself luxuriously, using the washcloth. She ran it over her shoulders and arm, then closed her eyes as she rubbed her breasts and nipples, then moved the cloth down over her belly until it was between her legs.

At that moment the door opened, and Archer stuck her head in.

"There you are," she said.

Roxy jerked the washcloth away from her crotch.

Archer entered, still naked.

"When did you discover there was a bathtub in here?"

"Just this morning," Roxy said. "I didn't sleep well and when I saw this, I realized I needed a bath."

"It looks lovely," Archer said.

"The water's cold, but you'll get used to it," Roxy said. "I'll be right out and you can run a bath for yourself."

"That's not necessary," Archer said. "I'll share yours. The tub looks big enough."

Before Roxy could say a word, Archer stepped into the tub and lowered herself into the water across from her.

Grinning, Archer held out her hand.

"Soap, please."

Roxy hesitated, then smiled back, laughed, splashed Archer and tossed her the soap.

"You're crazy," Roxy said.

Archer laughed and said, "Just a little."

***

They laughed and splashed in the tub like sisters, then got out and dried each other off. There was nothing sexual in the way they touched each other.

They got dressed and went down to the lobby, still laughing. They went to the dining room, which was almost deserted that early. A waiter showed them to a table and took their breakfast order.

"You look better," Archer said.

"Better than what?"

"Then when you first got up. Yeah, I was watchin' you."

"Why?"

"I was worried about you."

"Again," Roxy said, "why?"

"I thought I made you nervous last night," Archer said. "You know, with the nudity."

"So you jumped into the tub with me to loosen me up?"

"It worked, didn't it?"

"Yeah," Roxy said, with a laugh. "Because you're crazy."

"So are you, I think," Archer said. "That's why we get along."

"You're probably right."

The waiter brought their orders and they ate, telling each other stories they were now comfortable enough to share.

"How many men have you killed?" Archer asked, then.

"Too many," Roxy said. "And you?"

"More than that," Archer said. "I'm older than you."

"A few years."

Archer grinned.

"More than a few, but thanks."

When they finished, they sat over a final cup of coffee.

"Your father, the bounty hunter," Archer said. "Do you think he'd come after me? Is that why you're stickin' around me?"

"Well," Roxy sat back in her chair, "I never thought of that."

They laughed, again.

Chapter Nineteen

After breakfast they saddled their horses and rode them out of the livery. Outside they examined the street in all directions before starting to ride out. Of course, the three would-be bounty hunters from the day before didn't have to follow them out of town. Figuring they were heading for Arizona, they could have just waited along the way to ambush them.

That was why they weren't going to ride directly to Arizona.

As they rode out of the Amarillo city limits, Roxy said, "I suggest we take the long way."

"And which way is the long way?"

Roxy whistled and waved her finger.

"Roundabout," she said. "I'm expecting those three to try to ambush us."

"So we'll zig," Archer said, "and then zag, and then zig, again. And we'll avoid Tucumcari."

"Right."

***

In the middle of all the zigging and zagging Archer said, "Why wouldn't they just go to Millford and wait for us there, Roxy?"

"They would if they were smart and patient," Roxy replied. "If they took you near Millford, it would be an easy thing to collect the bounty."

"But you don't think they're smart?"

"Or patient," Roxy said.

"They were smart enough to back off," Archer pointed out.

"Because we backed them off," Roxy pointed out.

As it started to get dark Roxy said, "Okay, that's enough zigzag for today. Let's make camp."

Roxy saw to the horses while Archer made a fire. They decided Angel Eyes was a better cook than Lady Gunsmith, so she got a pot of coffee going and put a pan on the fire.

"How we doing?" Roxy asked, approaching the fire.

"We're gettin' there," Archer said. She dumped a can of beans into the pan.

Once they each had a cup of coffee and a pan of beans in their hands they sat back, relaxed, and ate.

"All right," Roxy said, "I suggest a change of plans."

"I'm listenin'."

"We stop zigging-and-zagging and head straight to Millford."

"So, a complete turnaround from what we were doin' before," Archer observed.

"Right."

"Why?"

"I think it'd be better if we got to Millford sooner than later," Roxy said. "Maybe even before those three."

"That suits me," Archer said. "I didn't much like all that . . . zaggin', as you called it."

"Why didn't you say something?"

Archer shrugged.

"I didn't have a better idea."

"You know," Roxy said, "this is your life we're trying to save."

"And you almost got killed once, already," Archer said. "I think we're both gonna breath a lot easier when we get this settled."

"You're probably right."

"But I'm with you," Archer said. "Let's just head straight for Millford and we'll handle whatever comes along."

They finished eating, cleaning the plates and made a fresh pot of coffee, then sat across the fire from each other, sipping.

"I'll take the first watch tonight," Archer said. "Wake you in four hours."

"Right."

"But before you turn in, I've been wonderin'," Arch-er said.

"About what?"

"Which one of us is faster."

"Does it matter?" Roxy asked.

"Tell me you ain't wondered the same thing."

"I gave it some thought," Roxy said. "But Like I said—"

"Yeah, yeah, it don't matter," Archer said. "I know . . . but I'm curious. Ain't you?"

Instead of answering, Roxy asked, "So what do you want to do about it?"

"I was thinkin'," Archer said, "tomorrow, before we get back on the trail, we have us a little contest."

"And if we do that, you'll stop thinking about it?" Roxy asked.

"Well," Archer admitted, "I guess that would depend on which one of us wins."

"You're not suggesting we shoot it out."

"No, not face-to-face," Archer said. "I'm talkin' about targets."

"Targets," Roxy said.

"Yeah," Archer said. "Like . . . tree branches. There's plenty of tree branches around here."

"Okay," Roxy said, "in the morning, after breakfast, target shooting. Then we'll get on the trail." She put her cup down. "I'm going to turn in."

"You do that," Archer said. "You'll need to be sharp in the mornin'."

Roxy stopped, gave Archer a look that made the blonde shrug, and then headed for her bedroll.

Chapter Twenty

Riding directly to Millford, Arizona seemed to do the trick. They arrived on the outskirts of town without having been ambushed along the way.

"They're likely to be waiting for us in town," Roxy said.

"Or they gave it up after we backed them off in Amarillo," Archer offered.

"That's a possibility, too," Roxy said, "one that I'm in favor of."

"Okay," Archer said, "so you ride in and see if you can collect the bounty with this." She handed Roxy her orange bandana. "I'll ride in later, after I do something to disguise myself."

"Like what?" Roxy asked. "That blonde hair's going to be like a shining star riding down main street."

"I'm gonna do somethin' with dirt."

"Dirt?"

Archer grinned and said, "You'll see."

"Okay, well, I'll check into the first hotel I come to, and see you there after I try the bank," Roxy said.

"If you get the five thousand," Archer said, "maybe we should just split it and light out. It would serve whoever put up the money."

"Why not?" Roxy agreed. "If they pay it, the bounty will be off you. But let's cross that bridge when we come to it."

"Okay," Archer said, "watch your back."

"Always."

Archer dismounted and filled both hands with dirt as Roxy rode toward town.

***

Roxy found Millford to be a mid-sized town, with several saloons and hotels. She stopped at the first hotel she came to and went inside. There were tables with people eating in the lobby, with the desk off to one side. As she approached the desk, diners in the room looked at her. The desk clerk, a mousy little man with the slightest mustache, smiled at her.

"Can I help you, Madam?"

"I'd like a room," she said, "and a meal."

"You can have both," the man said. "Please, sign in." Roxy signed in with her real name. "Your key. If you'd like to take your things to your room, I can have a meal waiting for you when you come down."

"I'd like to see to my horse first," she said, "but that'd be fine when I come back." She took the key. "I won't be long."

"Whenever you're ready Miss . . ." He read the register ". . . Doyle."

"Thank you. Can you tell me where the nearest livery stable is?"

"Just at the end of the street."

"Thank you."

Roxy left the hotel and started walking her horse to the end of the street.

***

As Roxy left, a man stood up from his table and walked to the desk.

"Did you say . . . Doyle?"

The clerk nodded and turned the register so the man could read it.

"Roxy Doyle, Mr. Turner," he said.

The man read the name and frowned.

"What's the Lady Gunsmith doin' in Millford?" Turner wondered aloud.

The clerk shrugged.

"What room did you give her?"

"Room eight, end of the hall."

The man went back to his table, where a second man was eating.

"Did you hear that?" Turner asked.

"I heard," Ben Logan said, chewing his steak. "Roxy Doyle."

"The Lady Gunsmith."

"Yes."

"What do you think she's doin' here?" Turner asked.

"Who knows? Maybe she's here to collect the bounty on Angel Eyes?"

"If she is, she'll have to come and see me," Turner said. "After all, I'm the president of the bank."

"Yes, you are," Logan said. "Which means you know who put that bounty on the head of Liz Archer."

"Do I?" Turner wiped his mouth with his napkin and stood up. "I better get back to my office in case she does show up." He looked at Logan. "Coming?"

"I'm going to finish my meal," Turner said. "I'll see you later."

"Whatever you say."

Turner left the hotel while Ben turned his attention back to his meal. Perhaps when Miss Doyle returned, he'd welcome her on behalf of the town.

Chapter Twenty-One

Roxy boarded her horse at the livery and returned to the hotel. The clerk nodded to her and pointed to a table. She assumed this meant when she came down, her meal would be ready. Before going up the stairs she noticed that many of the diners who had been there when she arrived were now gone.

Her room was small, but clean, which was more important to her than size. She walked to the window, saw that it overlooked the front street. Normally, she would have switched rooms, but she was interested in comings and goings.

She left her saddlebags and rifle on the bed and went back down to the lobby. As she suspected, her meal was on the table.

"Sorry, there's no menu," the clerk told her. "We only do one dish. Today it's beef stew."

"That's fine," she said. "Thank you."

She sat at the table and breathed in the aroma of the of stew, which was chock full of beef, carrots and potatoes. She took a taste and found it very good. Much better than the beans she and Archer had been eating for the past week or so on the trail.

The clerk brought her some more coffee.

"You're the desk clerk and the waiter?"

"Neither one keeps me real busy," the man admitted.

"Can you tell me where the bank is?"

"The Bank of Millford?" he asked.

"Is there another one?" Roxy asked.

"Uh, no," the clerk said, "no, there's only one. If you keep going past the livery, you'll come to it. The street curves."

"Thank you," she said.

"Enjoy your meal," he said, and returned to the front desk.

When she finished, she went to the desk to pay her check.

"The place has emptied out," she said. "I hope that has nothing to do with me."

"What?" the clerk said. "Oh, no, it's usually quiet this time of day."

"I see," she said. "Well, thanks for the stew." She stepped away, then turned back. "Oh, who do I ask for at the bank?"

"Um, for what?"

"Why, to collect the bounty on Angel Eyes."

"Oh," the clerk said, "that would be Mr. Turner, the bank president."

"Thanks, again."

She left the hotel and headed for the bank, wondering if Liz Archer was already somewhere in town?

***

When Roxy entered the bank there were no customers, and a single teller behind one of two cages.

"Can I help you, Miss?" the man asked. He was middle-aged, with wispy grey hairs sticking out from beneath his visor.

"Yes, I'd like to see the bank president."

"That would be Mr. Turner," the clerk said.

"That's what I was told."

"He'd be in his office."

She waited for him to say something else, then asked, "Could you tell him I'm here?"

"What's your name?"

"Roxy Doyle."

"And why do you want to see him?"

"To collect a bounty."

The man looked shocked.

"Oh my," the clerk said, "the bounty?"

"Yes," Roxy said, "the bounty on Angel Eyes."

"Oh, yes," the clerk said. "Of course. I'll let him know you're here."

The man turned and walked to the door marked PRESIDENT. He knocked and entered, soon reappearing.

"You can go in, Miss," he said.

"Thank you."

As soon as she entered, she recognized the man behind the desk as one of the diners in the hotel.

"Miss Doyle?" He came around the desk. "I'm Justin Turner, the bank president. Delighted to meet you."

He shook her hand firmly.

"Please, have a seat."

Roxy took the chair in front of the man's desk, while he returned to his.

"Now, what can I do for you?"

"As I told your teller," she said, "I'm here to collect the bounty." She produced the poster and laid it on his desk.

"Ah yes," he said, "the five thousand dollars."

"That's right."

"I assume you have proof?"

She took the orange bandana from her pocket and put it down on the desk.

"This is your proof?"

"She always wore it," Roxy said.

"And you took it off her body?"

"I did."

The man sat back in his chair.

"You're the Lady Gunsmith, right?"

"That's right."

"And you outdrew Angel Eyes?"

"I did."

"I wish I could have seen that," he said.

"What did you have against her?" Roxy asked.

"I'm sorry."

"To offer such a bounty," she went on, "it must've been personal."

"I never met the woman," Turner said. "Had nothing against her. I just run a bank."

"Then who did put that bounty on her head?" Roxy asked.

"Oh, I can't tell you that, Miss Doyle," Turner said. "We don't talk about our depositors."

"But this is more than just a depositor," she said. "This is someone paying to have someone killed. That's an odd thing for a bank to be involved in."

"But we're not involved," Turner said. "We're just holding the money until someone collects it."

"Like me."

"Well, yes," Turner said, "but I'm afraid I'm going to need more proof than this." He indicated the orange bandana. "Lots more."

Chapter Twenty-Two

"What more would you like?" she asked. "An ear?"

"Nothing so elaborate," he said. "A telegram from the law in whatever town you were in when you, uh, killed her."

"What about a story from the local newspaper, there?" she asked.

"That would do, as well."

Roxy studied the man for a moment. She could have taken her gun out at that point, stuck it in his face and forced him to talk, but she decided to wait. After all, even with a gun pointed at him the man could lie.

Roxy expected Archer to put in an appearance very soon. Together they could hatch a plan, possibly just follow Mr. Turner to whoever put up the money.

"Well," she said, "then I'd better get to it. Do you have a telegraph office?"

"I'm sorry, no," he said. "The nearest one is in the next town over, called Iverville."

"How far is that?"

"Thirty miles."

"Then I'd better get started."

"Would you like this back?" he asked, picking up the bandana.

"Yes, I would. Thank you."

He walked her to the office door.

"I'll see you when you have your proof," he said.

"Yes," she said, "you will."

She left the office, and the bank, tempted to go right back in and stick the gun in his face.

***

Roxy returned to her hotel to see if Liz Archer had arrived. She was curious as to what disguiser the blonde had chosen.

As she entered she saw all the dining room tables empty, and the clerk lounging behind the desk. When he saw Roxy he straightened up.

"Can I do something for you, Miss?" he asked. "Did you find the bank?"

"I did, thank you," she said. "I'm going to my room, now, so there's nothing else you can do for me."

"Yes, Miss."

Roxy went up to her room and hesitated a moment. She drew her gun before inserting the key and unlocking it. She swung the door open and waited.

"How'd you know I was here?" Liz Archer asked, from inside.

"Instinct," Roxy said, stepping through the door.

There was a single chair in the room, and Archer was sitting in it. That pleased Roxy, because the girl was too dirty to sit on the bed. Her blonde hair was black with sand, as were her face and clothes. No one would have recognized her as the infamous Angel Eyes—except, of course, for those luminous blue eyes.

Roxy holstered her gun and closed the door.

"Did you go to the bank and get the money?" Archer asked.

"I saw the bank president," Roxy said, "but I don't have the money."

"Why not?"

"He said the bandana wasn't proof enough," Roxy said. "He needed to hear from a lawman or read a newspaper."

"How do we do either of those?"

"We don't," Roxy said. "You follow him. He's got to tell somebody I wasn't here claiming the bounty."

Archer shrugged.

"So we follow him."

"Not we," Roxy said, "you."

"Why me?"

"Because," Roxy said, "you're filthy and no one will recognize you."

"I was hoping to wash this off."

"That can come later," Roxy said. "Before you get clean, let's make sure you're safe."

Chapter Twenty-Three

After Roxy described her encounter with Turner, they decided Archer would take up a position outside the bank and then follow the bank president, wherever he went. Roxy gave her directions to the bank.

"Even if he sees you, he won't look twice," Roxy said.

"All this dirt makes me itch," Archer complained. "I wish we'd changed places."

"Well," Roxy said, "you couldn't very well have tried to collect the bounty on yourself."

"I guess I better get over there before the bank closes," Archer said, standing.

Roxy looked Archer over and said, "You're going to need some new clothes after this."

"Ah," Archer said, "somethin' to look forward to." She went to the door, opened it and turned. "I'll go out the same way I came in, the back."

"I'll stay alert," Roxy promised. "At the first sound of shots, I'll come running."

"Hopefully," Archer said, "in time."

***

Roxy Doyle Meets an Angel

Roxy waited ten minutes for Archer to get away, then went back downstairs, through the lobby and to the front. She looked around, saw a wicker armchair off to one side. She dragged it closer to the door and sat down to wait.

**

Archer went out the back and followed Roxy's directions to the bank. When she arrived, she chose a doorway across the street, of a store that had already closed for the day, and settled in to wait. She didn't think it could be long, since it was almost five o'clock.

A small man came out of the bank at five-oh-five and walked briskly away. Undoubtedly, this was the teller Roxy told her about. Archer watched him until he disappeared down the street then turned her eyes back to the bank door.

At five-thirty-five another man came out, fitting Roxy's description of the bank president. The man locked the door, then turned and glanced both ways before starting off in the opposite direction the teller had gone.

Foot traffic at that time of day was light, as most businesses were either closed or closing. Citizens were either home having supper, or in a saloon. But the few on the street paid no attention to the dirty urchin.

She remained on the opposite side of the street, slightly behind him. He was striding purposely without ever looking back. Finally, he reached the livery stable and went inside. Archer expected him to come out on horseback, which meant she'd have to run in and get hers. But instead he came out in a buggy, being drawn by a single horse. As he headed out of town, she went inside.

"Back so soon?" the hostler asked, cringing a bit at her appearance.

"No time," Archer said. "I'll saddle my horse myself."

She hurriedly did so while the hostler watched, then walked it out of its stall.

"The man who just left in a buggy," she said.

"Bennett, the bank president."

"Did he say where he was goin'?"

"Not a word," the man said. "Rushed in, hitched up his buggy, and drove out."

She looked at the ground, saw the tracks left by the buggy wheels. One wheel seemed to have a slight cut in it.

"Those his tracks?"

"They are."

"Thanks."

She mounted up and rode out, turning in the direction the bank president had gone. There was no need to chase him, as his tracks were very easy to follow.

***

The Bank president and Archer had walked past the hotel, and the seated Roxy, without paying her any attention. When they had both gone by and decided to do more than just sit. She stood and followed in their wake.

She didn't see Turner come out of the stable, but she did see a mounted Archer, who looked like a dusty urchin on horseback. She decided to follow.

Inside the livery the hostler turned and gaped at her as she entered.

"Busy day," he commented. "Should I saddle your horse?"

Feeling no rush, she said, "Please."

While he did, she studied the fresh tracks on the floor made by buggy wheels and Archer's horse.

"Here you go," he said, walking her horse over and handing her the reins.

"Thank you." She mounted up. "Any idea where that dusty woman was going?"

"She was following the bank president, in his bug-gy," the man said. "Maybe she's thinkin' of robbin' him."

"Is that something you'd want to tell the sheriff?" she asked.

"Oh, no," he said. "All she'd get is his own money. And he'd deserve it."

"You don't like him?"

The man smiled.

"Nobody does."

"Thanks for the information," she said.

She rode out of the livery and turned in the direction the buggy and Archer had taken.

Chapter Twenty-Four

Justin Turner reined in his horse and buggy in front of the ranch house. When he stepped down, he handed the reins to a ranch hand.

"Where's the boss?" he asked.

"Detmer's in the bunkhouse—"

"No, not the foreman," the bank president said, cutting him off, "the boss."

"Oh, I think he's in the house."

"Keep the rig here, I won't be long," Turner instructed.

"Yes, sir."

He went up the steps to the front door, started to open it, then decided to knock. When a tall, older man opened the door he said, "We have to talk."

"You might as well come in, then," the man said.

Turner entered the house and then closed the door.

***

From a distance Archer watched, saw the man who had opened the door, but not well enough to see if she knew him. As the door closed, she heard something behind her, turned and saw Roxy.

"I thought I was supposed to follow him," she said.

"You did," Roxy said, and I decided to follow you instead of just waiting. Where is he?"

"He went inside."

Both women turned their attention to the house. Roxy took in the whole picture of the house, barn, corral, and ranch hands.

"I wonder whose ranch this is?" she said.

"We could go down there and ask 'em," Archer replied.

"It's probably not a good idea to let them know you're here," Roxy pointed out.

"All right," Archer said, "you go down and ask."

"I'm supposed to be out of town, trying to get my proof that you're dead."

"Then you'll catch them off guard, won't you?"

Roxy waited a moment, then said, "I think you're right."

She turned to go to her horse.

"I wasn't—I was only half serious," Archer said.

"Just keep watching," Roxy said. "I'll go down and meet whoever owns this ranch and find out if he put up the bounty."

"Why else would the bank president be here?" Archer called out.

"Exactly," Roxy called back, mounting up.

***

The ranch hand standing by Turner's buggy looked stunned by the beauty of the woman riding toward him. He had never seen a woman like her before. A few of the other hands near the corral stopped what they were doing to watch her ride by.

When she reined in her horse in front of him, he wasn't able to speak. He just stared.

"Hello," Roxy said, to wake him.

"Huh? Oh, uh, hello, Miss."

"Do you mind if I ask who owns this ranch?"

"Huh? Oh, sure, that'd be the boss, Mister Lewis."

"Lewis?"

"Randolph Lewis," the man said.

"Has he ever—"

"For more questions you'd have to talk to the foreman, Kyle Detmer."

"And where's he?"

"In the bunkhouse."

Roxy considered whether she should go into the house, or the bunkhouse. She decided to keep the banker from knowing she was there, just yet, and walked to the bunkhouse. As she approached a tall, rangy man in his late thirties came out. When he saw her, he stopped and waited.

"Is Mr. Detmer inside?" she asked.

"I'm Detmer," he said. "Can I help you?"

"You're the foreman?"

"That's right."

"You seem young for the job."

"Do I?" he asked, smoking. "I'm forty-two. That feels old, to me."

"You look younger."

"Thanks," he said. "But what can I do for you?"

"Do you know about the bounty that's been put on the head of Liz Archer, Angel Eyes?"

"I've heard of it," he said. "Why?"

"I came to town to claim it," she said, "but the banker's being sketchy about it."

"You mean Turner," Detmer said. "Yeah, he's a little . . . sneaky."

"He's here, right now," she said. "With your boss. Did Mr. Lewis put that bounty out there?"

"If he did, that's not somethin' I'd know," Detmer said. "I run the ranch. I don't have anything to do with his other business. Now if you'll excuse me, I have work to do. If you have any more questions, you can ask Mr. Lewis."

He strode away.

Chapter Twenty-Five

Roxy walked back to the house and saw that the banker's buggy was gone. The cowhand she had spoken to was still standing by her horse.

"Mr. Turner left?" she asked.

"Just now," he said. "Are you leavin'?"

Roxy looked out to where she knew Liz Archer was waiting and watching.

"No," she said, "I think I'll go inside."

"To see Mr. Lewis?"

"That's right."

"Did Kyle say it was okay?"

Roxy smiled at the cowhand.

"He suggested it."

The young man looked surprised.

"I guess it's okay, then."

"Thanks."

She went up the steps and knocked on the front door.

"Mr. Lewis?" she asked the man who opened it.

"Yes?"

"Can I talk to you?"

"That depends," he said. "Who are you?"

"Roxy Doyle."

"Ah, Miss Doyle," Lewis said. "Yes, come in."

He allowed her to enter, closed the door and then showed her the way to an office.

"Please, have a seat," he said, going around behind his desk.

Roxy sat across from him.

"Were you expecting me?" she asked.

"Not exactly," Lewis said. "Mr. Turner was just here and told me you were in town."

"He was here about the bounty?"

"What bounty would that be?"

"The five-thousand dollars you put out on the head of Liz Archer."

"Who?"

"You know, Angel Eyes."

He shook his head and said, "I don't know what you're talking about, Miss Doyle. Why would I put out a bounty on anyone's head?"

"That's what I'm here to find out."

"You said you were in town to collect the bounty?"

"I didn't say that."

"Yes, you did."

"No, the bank president must have told you that," she said.

"No," Lewis said, "you told me that when I answered the door."

Roxy could see he wasn't going to admit to putting up the bounty.

"Well," she said, "I've taken up enough of your time. You have a ranch to run. And I guess you have other businesses."

"What makes you say that"

"You're a rich rancher," she said. "And your foreman said he runs your ranch, but isn't involved in your other businesses."

"When did you speak to Kyle?"

"Just before I came to you."

"Well, he's right," Lewis said. "He runs my ranch, that's all."

They both stood.

"I'll walk you out."

They went to the front door together, which Lewis opened for her.

"Thanks for your time, Mr. Lewis."

"You're welcome, Miss Doyle."

She left the house, went down the steps. The young cowhand who had been watching her horse was gone, but the foreman, Kyle Detmer, was there.

"Nice horse," he said.

"It's just a horse."

Detmer rubbed the horse's nose.

"No name?"

"No."

"Too bad," the foreman said. "Can I help you mount?"

"I can make it on my own, thanks," she told him.

He watched as she mounted up.

"I'll be in town tomorrow," he said. "Why don't we have supper together?"

"Why?"

"I might have some information for you," he said.

"I'll look forward to it, then," she said, and rode off.

***

When she reached Archer, the blond woman was grinning.

"What's funny?" Roxy asked.

"Who was that fella by your horse?"

"A young cowhand—"

"No, not him," Archer interrupted, "the second one."

"Oh," Roxy said, "that's the foreman. I'm having supper with him tomorrow."

"That was fast work."

"He said he might have some information for me."

"From here he looked pretty handsome," Archer commented.

"Huh," Roxy said, "I didn't notice. Come on, let's ride back to town and get you a bath."

"Now that sounds good," Archer said.

Chapter Twenty-Six

When they got back to town, Roxy arranged a bath with the desk clerk, then sneaked Archer into the room and stood watch on the door.

By the time Archer got out of the bathtub, the water was more mud than anything else. Roxy was able to sneak her back up to the hotel room.

"One bed?" Archer asked. "That'll be interestin'."

"Don't start again," Roxy said. "The bed's big enough for the both of us."

Archer sat on the bed, still drying her hair with a towel. She was wearing a clean shirt and jeans.

"So," she said, "tell me about this foreman. He looked tall and fit from a distance."

"From close up, too," Roxy said.

"Ah, so you did notice."

"I noticed."

"Is he handsome?"

"In a rugged sort of way."

"Ah," Archer said, "I like that."

"We'll have to keep our minds on business, Liz," Roxy said. "The business of getting this bounty off your head."

"I'm all for that," Archer said. "How do you propose we do that?"

"First we have to prove that Mr. Lewis is the man who put the price *on* your head."

"You asked him, didn't you?"

"I did."

"And he said he didn't do it."

"He did," Roxy said.

"Then how do we prove it?"

"We'll start by seeing what the foreman has to say," Roxy said.

"You think he'll give up his boss?"

"I don't know what's on his mind," Roxy admitted. "The first time I spoke to him he was very clear. He runs the ranch and doesn't know anything else. Then, when I came out of the house, he was there, and willing to talk."

"At supper."

"Right."

"But he didn't say what he wanted to talk about."

"No he didn't."

"Well, Roxy, you know men as well as I do," Archer said. "What do you think he wants?"

"I'll find out for sure tomorrow."

***

They slept in the same bed, and out of mutual respect, each wore a shirt rather than being naked. When they woke, they took turns washing and dressing.

"Well," Archer said, "I suppose I have to stay in this room all day. What will you do?"

"I don't know," Roxy said. "I have time to kill before my supper with the foreman."

"Where are you supposed to meet him?"

"We didn't really say," Roxy replied, "but I figure he'll come to the hotel."

"Have you made contact with the law, here?" Archer asked.

"Not yet," Roxy said. "I suppose that should be my next stop."

"After breakfast?"

"Of course."

"What do you think would happen if we were seen having breakfast together?" Archer asked

"I think that's a good idea," Roxy said. "Why don't we find out?"

Archer picked up her gunbelt and strapped it on.

"That sounds better than sittin' in this room all day."

***

119

They walked across the lobby to the hotel dining room. At that moment, the lobby was empty, but the desk clerk stared after them with his mouth open.

When they reached the door of the dining room a waiter appeared.

"Breakfast, ladies?"

"Yes, please," Roxy said.

"This way."

The room was empty, but he showed them to a table near the back, which suited them. They sat so they both could see the door.

"What can I get for you ladies?"

"Ham-and-eggs," Archer said.

"The same," Roxy said. "And coffee."

"Coming up."

He came with the coffee first, and then their plates. By the time they were eating, several others had entered and been seated. They drew some curious looks, but the diners quickly turned their attention to their own meals.

"Nobody looks particularly interested in us," Archer observed.

"They're probably also guests," Roxy said. "Maybe some locals might be more interested. We can take a stroll through town."

"After breakfast," Archer said.

"Definitely."

Chapter Twenty-Seven

They stopped just outside the hotel.

"This is a change in tactics," Archer said. "First I ride into town in disguise, and now I walk down main street, bold as brass."

"Lewis has to be the man who put the price on your head," Roxy said. "Why else would the bank president ride out to see him after my visit."

"That sounds right," Archer said. "Once word gets out that I'm here, somebody's bound to try to collect. Especially when it becomes known that you lied."

"I was going to make contact with the local law," Roxy said. "Why don't we just do that together? Then for sure word will get around that you're alive and in town."

"Sounds good to me," Archer said. "I'd rather take action than just sit and wait."

"So let's do it."

***

They only had to walk a few more blocks before coming to the sheriff's office. They approached the front door and stopped.

J.R. Roberts

"Why do I get the feelin' we don't know what we're doin'?" Archer asked.

Roxy laughed

They opened the door and entered the office. A man seated behind a desk looked up and raised his eyebrows. He was in his forties, with a bushy mustache and grey-streaked hair.

"Ladies," he said. "What can I do for you?"

"Sheriff—"

"Pike," the man said, "Sheriff Carl Pike."

"Sheriff Pike, I'm Roxy Doyle—"

"Lady Gunsmith," the man interrupted.

"May I finish talking?"

"Sorry," Pike said. "Go ahead, Miss Doyle."

"This is Liz Archer," Roxy said, "also known as Angel Eyes."

"When did the two of you get to town?" he asked.

"Yesterday," Roxy said.

"And what brings you here?"

"I think you know," Roxy said. "You must know. We're here about the price on her head."

Pike smiled and looked at Archer.

"You want to collect the price on your own head?"

"It's an idea," Archer said, "but no. We're here to confront the man who placed the price on my head."

"And you know who that is?" Pike asked.

"We have a good idea," Roxy said. "I spoke to the bank president yesterday, and he immediately rode out to the ranch of Randolph Lewis."

"Mr. Lewis?" Pike repeated. "You think he put the bounty out?"

"It's a good bet," Roxy said. "What we'd like to find out is why."

"Did you think I'd know?"

"You *are* the sheriff," Roxy said. "We kind of hoped."

"Well," Pike said, "I'm sorry to disappoint you. I've heard of this bounty, but I have no idea who's responsible. And if it's Randolph Lewis, it's a surprise to me."

"At least," Roxy said, "we gave it a try. Thanks for your time."

They started for the door.

"Aren't you takin' a chance?" the sheriff asked.

"A chance?" Roxy asked.

Pike pointed at Archer.

"If there's a price on your head, you're takin' a chance by walkin' around."

"I hid yesterday," she said. "I'm tired of hidin'."

"I guess you know what you're doing," Pike said.

"Let's hope so," Archer said, and followed Roxy out the door.

***

Roxy and Archer walked back toward their hotel, staying alert and watching each other's back. Along the way they encountered a small café and decided to go in and have a meal. Archer was still hungry after their time on the trail, despite the breakfast they'd had.

"Now what?" Archer asked, when they both had plates in front of them.

Archer had gone for a big steak, but Roxy had a small bowl of stew, since she was to have supper with Kyle Detmer.

"Well," Roxy said, "we could just sit here and wait for somebody to take a shot at us."

"Making a staked goat of myself has never been one of my favorite pastimes," Archer replied.

"Then I'll just wait for Mr. Detmer to take me to supper and see what's on his mind."

"You really think he might give up his boss?" Archer said. "Or is he just plannin' to get you into bed?"

"Might be both those things," Roxy said.

"And just which of those things are you looking for?" Archer asked, arching one eyebrow.

"Who knows?" Roxy replied. "Maybe both."

Chapter Twenty-Eight

After the meal, they decided Roxy would sit out in front of the hotel while Archer went back to the room.

"I'll wait for Detmer to get here," Roxy said. "Hopefully, it's not too early. I'm really not hungry, after that stew."

"Don't worry about it," Archer said. "I think a meal is the last thing on his mind."

"I wouldn't mind a piece of pie."

"I think he's more interested in a piece of—"

"Just go to the room, Liz," Roxy said, cutting her off.

Archer smiled and said, "Okay, but stay alert. I'll be out here at the first sound of a shot."

"Let's remember which one of us has the price on her head," Roxy said.

But, as Archer went into the hotel, Roxy knew there didn't have to be a price on her head for someone to take a shot at Lady Gunsmith. And she didn't have to be told to stay alert.

***

The banker, Justin Turner, stayed out of sight, but could see from the front window of the bank, Roxy Doyle sitting in front of the hotel. He had also seen her and a blonde woman leave the hotel and return. It was fairly obvious to him that Doyle had not killed Angel Eyes, but was working with her to find out who put the price on her head. If both women came to him with their guns out, he was prepared to tell them. But he fervently hoped that wouldn't happen. Maybe the rancher, Lewis, would take some sort of action before something like that could happen.

Just before closing he went back to the window and saw that Doyle hadn't moved. What was she waiting for? That was when he saw Kyle Detmer ride into town. Hopefully, the foreman had been sent by his boss to take some kind of action.

He watched as the foreman reined in his horse in front of the hotel and dismounted . . .

***

Roxy remained seated as the foreman dismounted.

"You're waitin' for me," Detmer said, with a smile.

"Let's just say I'm waiting," Roxy corrected.

"Well," he said, "I'm ready for some supper. Will you join me?"

"Why not?" she asked, standing. "You're paying, right?"

"Of course," he said. "I invited you."

"Where are we going?" she asked.

"It's a short walk," Detmer said. "I'll leave my horse here."

He led the way in the opposite direction of the sheriff's office and the café where she and Archer had eaten earlier.

It was only a few blocks when they came to a restaurant that looked very busy.

"Looks like a popular place," Roxy said.

"Best restaurant in town," Detmer said.

"Do you eat here often?"

"Once in a while," he said, "but I wanted to impress you."

They entered and a waiter took them to an available table. It wasn't in an ideal location for Roxy, but she made sure Detmer sat with his back to the door.

"Everything here is good, so you can't go wrong," he told her.

The waiter gave them menus and said he would return. When he came back, he carried two glasses and a pitcher of cold water.

"Ready to order?" he asked.

"Ladies first," Detmer said.

"Roast chicken," Roxy said. She was surprised to find herself hungry for more than a piece of pie.

"A steak for me," Detmer said.

"Comin' up."

"So," Roxy said, "does your boss know you're here?"

"He knows I eat supper," Detmer said. "He doesn't always know where."

"I mean," Roxy said, "does he know you're here, with me. Did he tell you to talk to me?"

"What? No," Detmer said. "He didn't. *I* wanted to talk to you."

"Why?"

"Do you really think my boss put the bounty on Liz Archer's head?"

"Yes."

"And you didn't come here to collect it?"

"No," Roxy said, "Liz is still alive."

"And here?"

"Yes."

He sat back in his chair.

"I don't like working for a man who is hiring murderers."

"He didn't exactly hire anybody," Roxy said. "But he likely put that bounty on her."

"Same thing," Detmer said. "For a while, now, I've been thinkin' about quittin' my job and movin' on. This confirms it."

"You're quitting?"

"If it turns out he offered the bounty, yeah," Detmer said. "I ain't gonna work for a murderer."

"That speaks very highly of you, Mr. Detmer."

He grinned at her and said, "Call me Kyle."

Chapter Twenty-Nine

"So tell me," Roxy said, while they ate, "what connection could your boss have with Angel Eyes?"

"I have no idea," Detmer said.

"Could she have killed some relative of his?"

"He has no relatives."

"No wife?"

"She died long ago."

"No children?"

"A son, but he died.

"How?"

Detmer shrugged.

"He doesn't talk about that stuff with me."

"No one living?"

"He has a young granddaughter who lives with him."

"How young?"

"Fourteen or fifteen."

"Where's her mother?"

"After his son died, she left Lisa with him. He hasn't had any contact since."

They finished their meal and Detmer said, "Dessert? They make great pie."

"I think I'm full enough," Roxy said, "but you go ahead."

Detmer waved the waiter over and said, "Cherry pie."

"Comin' up, sir. With coffee?"

"Yes," Detmer said, "two."

The waiter nodded.

"I have a sweet tooth," Detmer said to Roxy. "I love cherry pie. I hope you don't mind I ordered you coffee."

"No, not at all," Roxy said. "Coffee's fine."

The waiter brought the coffee and pie and Detmer dug in.

"Want a bite?" he asked. "It's really good."

"Just one bite."

He held a forkful out to her. She leaned in and captured it.

"Oops," he said, and reached across the table to wipe the corner of her mouth with his thumb. "There."

"Thank you," she said. "Kyle, I thought you had something you wanted to talk to me about."

"I did," he said. "I wanted to know for sure if Mr. Lewis put the price on Angel Eyes' head. What did you think I had to say?"

"I thought you were going to tell me he did it."

"I'm sorry I can't do that," Detmer said. "What'll you do now?"

"Is there anyone else who knows about Mr. Lewis' business?"

"Yeah," Detmer said. "His lawyer, Ben Winchell."

"And where do I find him?"

"He has an office here in town."

"Would you introduce me?"

"Sure," Detmer said. "Can I finish my pie first?"

Roxy smiled and said, "Absolutely."

***

They left the restaurant and walked to the office of Benjamin Winchell, Attorney-at-Law.

"How well do you know him?" Roxy asked.

"Not well," Detmer said. "I've seen him from time to time when he comes out to the ranch."

"Will he be surprised to see you here?"

"I think he'll be more surprised to see you," Detmer said. "Let's go in."

They entered the office, found an empty secretary's desk in an outer office.

"That's his office," Detmer said, pointing to another door. He walked to it and knocked.

"Come in!" a voice called.

Detmer opened the door and allowed Roxy to precede him.

"Kyle," the man behind a desk said. "Is Mr. Lewis all right?"

"He's fine, Mr. Winchell."

"And who's this?"

Winchell stood, revealing himself to be about six-and-a-half feet tall. He appeared to be in his fifties.

"This is Roxy Doyle," Detmer said. "She has a few questions for you."

"Is that right?" He looked at Roxy. "Please, have a seat."

"I'll just wait outside," Detmer said, and backed out of the room.

"What's on your mind, Miss Doyle?" Winchell asked.

"Randolph Lewis," Roxy said.

"What about him?"

"Do you know about the price on the head of Liz Archer, otherwise known as Angel Eyes?"

"The lady gunfighter," Winchell said, "yes, I've heard something about that. What does that mean to you?"

"Do you know who I am?"

The man sat back in his chair.

"Yes, I've heard of you, too," he said. "Lady Gunsmith. But what does this have to do with Angel Eyes?"

"I've been mistaken for her, and shot at," Roxy said. "I didn't like it. So I'm trying to find out who put the price on her head, and why."

Winchell stared at her, then sat forward.

"You think Randolph Lewis put the price on her head?"

"I do."

"But . . . why?"

"That's what I wanted to ask you."

Chapter Thirty

"Why on earth would Randolph Lewis put a price on anyone's head?" the lawyer asked.

"That's what I'm asking you."

"If he did," Winchell asked, "why would I know?"

"You're his lawyer," Roxy said. "Don't you know all his business dealings?"

"Yes, I do," he said, "and none of them concern putting a bounty on anyone's head."

"What if it's not business?" Roxy asked. "What if it's personal?"

"Then I really wouldn't have any idea," Winchell said. "As you said, I'm involved in his business dealings, not in his personal life."

"Aren't you friends?"

"I don't think Randolph Lewis has any friends," Winchell said. "I'm just his lawyer."

Roxy was frustrated.

"I think you have to go another way, Miss Doyle," the lawyer said. "Find somebody else who knows Randolph Lewis' business or start looking in another direction."

"No," she said, "when I went to the bank president about the bounty, he went right to Mr. Lewis."

"Then maybe Turner knows more than he's saying."

"Or you do," Roxy said.

"I'm sorry," he said, "I've got nothing to tell you."

Roxy stood up.

"If you see your client," she said, "tell him Liz Archer and I won't stand still for this. Either lift the bounty, or he'll be sorry."

"I can tell him you said that," Winchell said. "But it doesn't do any good if he didn't put up that bounty in the first place."

"He did," Roxy said. "You tell him we know he did. In fact, tell him we'll both be out to see him, soon."

"Is that a threat?" Winchell asked.

"It's just a message," Roxy said. "Thanks for your time."

She turned and left the office, leaving the lawyer seated at his desk, frowning.

***

Kyle Detmer was waiting outside for Roxy.

"So?" the foreman asked.

"He claims not to know anything about a bounty," Roxy told him.

"So where do you go from here?"

"I'm not sure," she said. "I pretty much committed Liz and me to going out to see your boss, again."

"Why do that?"

"To let her face him," Roxy said. "Who knows, maybe she'll recognize him."

"You think my boss might have a former life?"

"Who knows?" she said. "How long have you known him?"

"I've worked for him for three years," Detmer said. "I didn't know him before that. He was looking for a foreman, and he hired me."

"Just like that?"

"I had experience," Detmer said.

"Well," she said, "thank you for supper, and for the introduction."

"I'm sorry I can't do more," Detmer said. "But . . . I'd like to see you again. Another supper?"

"Maybe," she said. "If I'm still here."

They walked back to the hotel and Detmer mounted his horse.

"If you and Miss Archer come to the ranch, ask for me," he said.

"We will."

"Then I'll see you again."

Roxy watched him ride away, then went up to the hotel room.

"You're not radiant," Archer said, as she walked in.

"What?"

"I thought after sex with the foreman you'd look radiant."

"We had an early supper, not sex," Roxy said.

"Too bad," Archer said. They both sat on the bed. "What did he have to say?"

"Nothing," Roxy said. "He doesn't know anything."

"He *says* he doesn't know anything, which could be a lie."

"Well," Roxy said, "he did introduce me to the rancher's lawyer."

"And?"

"And he also says he doesn't know anything."

"Everybody's lyin'," Archer said.

"Probably."

"So what now?"

"I think we should ride out to the ranch," Roxy said. "Maybe when you see him this'll all become clear."

"You think his name isn't Lewis?"

Roxy shrugged.

"Who knows," she said. "Maybe when you see him, you'll recognize him from somewhere."

"Okay," Archer said. "When do we go?"

Chapter Thirty-One

The next morning Roxy and Liz Archer rode out to Randolph Lewis' ranch. As they reined in their horses, the foreman, Kyle Detmer, came walking toward them from the barn.

"You told me to ask for you," Roxy reminded him.

"I thought I'd save you the trouble." He looked at Archer. "Hello, Miss Archer."

"Mr. Detmer."

"I assume you're here to see Mr. Lewis."

"That's right," Roxy said. "We want to see if Liz knows him. Then she can figure out why he wants her dead."

"Or if he's even the man who wants her dead," Detmer said.

"That, too."

"All right," Detmer said. "I'll take you in to see him. Follow me."

They tied off their horses and followed Detmer to the front door. Once there, he turned and looked at them.

"You're not gonna kill 'im, are you? And me?"

"Killing either one of you is not the plan," Roxy told him. "Right, Liz?"

"Right."

"Okay, then," Detmer said, and knocked on the door.

The door was opened by a young girl, about fourteen years old.

"Hello, Kyle."

"Lisa," Detmer said, "I've got two ladies here to see your grandfather. Is he home?"

"He is," she said. "He's doin' paperwork."

"Can we bother him?"

She smiled, which made her prettier.

"Sure," she said. "He hates paperwork. Come on in and I'll let him know you're here."

Detmer let Roxy and Archer precede him, then entered and closed the door. The girl, Lisa, disappeared into the house, then reappeared.

"He says you can go back, Kyle," she said. "And bring the ladies. You know the way."

"Yes, Lisa, I do."

She smiled at him and went to another part of the house.

"She likes you," Archer said.

"She's a kid," he said, "and she's my boss' granddaughter. This way."

Detmer led them to another room at the back of the house. An older man sat behind a desk and looked up as they appeared in the doorway.

Roxy Doyle Meets an Angel

"Mr. Lewis," Detmer said, "meet Roxy Doyle and Liz Archer."

The man stared at them.

"Liz?" Roxy asked.

"I don't know 'im," Archer said.

"Why would she know me?" Lewis asked.

"Because you put a price on her head," Roxy replied.

"What?" He looked at his foreman. "What is this woman talking about?"

"There's a price on Miss Archer's head," Detmer said. "There's already been a couple of attempts to collect."

"What's that got to do with me?"

"Instructions are for the price to be collected at the Millford Bank," Roxy said. "When I went to the bank and talked to Mr. Turner about it, he immediately rode out here to talk with you."

"That's not unusual," Lewis said, "seeing as how I own the bank." He looked at Archer. "But that doesn't mean I put a price on this young lady's head." Then he looked at Detmer again. "Why did you bring them here?"

"To prove to them that you didn't do it," the foreman replied.

"I was hoping Liz would recognize you," Roxy said. "I guess we were wrong."

J.R. Roberts

"You certainly were," Lewis said. "Miss Archer, I'm certainly sorry that you are in danger because of this price, but I assure you, I had nothing to do with it."

"I understand, Sir," Archer said. "Thanks for seeing us."

"Kyle," Lewis said, "show these young ladies out."

"Yes, sir."

"Then come back," the man went on. "We need to talk."

"Yes, sir."

The foreman ushered them from the room and led them to the front door.

When they got to their horses Detmer said, "Well, I hope that satisfies you."

"Not exactly," Archer said. "We still need to find out who's behind this price on my head."

"I wish I could help," Detmer said. "As it is, I think I might be gettin' fired."

He went back into the house as they mounted up.

"So?" Archer asked, as they rode away. "Are you satisfied Lewis didn't do it?"

"Maybe he didn't do it," Roxy said, "but I'll bet he knows who did."

"And what makes you say that?"

"You heard what he said," Roxy pointed out. "He owns the bank."

Chapter Thirty-Two

When Roxy and Archer got back to town, they reined in their horses in front of a saloon called The Ten of Clubs and went inside. There were only a few customers that time of day. They went to the bar, got a beer each, and carried them to a table.

"So maybe Lewis isn't behind the price," Archer said, "but he's probably behind the money. That's what you're saying?"

"It's his bank," Roxy said, "so it's his money."

"Then why did we leave without asking him?"

"Because he would've lied."

"So what do you suggest?" Archer asked.

"We watch."

"Who?"

"One of us can watch the bank manager, Turner, while the other one watches Lewis."

"And what do we expect to see?" Archer asked. "Nobody's gonna claim the money, because nobody's killed me . . . yet. You already tried that, and you followed Turner out to Lewis' ranch. And now we're back where we started."

"So what do you suggest?"

"Well, we've got to do something before somebody else tries to collect." Archer shook her head. "I just don't know what."

They took a moment while Roxy went to the bar and came back with two fresh beers.

"I know what I'd like to do," Archer said.

"And what's that?"

"Put a bullet in the fucker's head."

"Lewis?"

"Who else?"

"You think that would stop the bounty from being paid?" Roxy asked.

"Tell you the truth," Archer said, "I don't know. But he won't see it paid."

"I can't just murder him, Liz," Roxy said. "No matter what my reputation says. Or yours, neither."

Archer frowned, unhappily.

"I know," she said. "I just said I'd like to do it that way."

"So since that won't happen." Roxy said, "let's think of something else."

"And drink," Archer said.

***

Roxy and Archer were on their third beer each and had managed to fend off two attempts each to engage them. The men they rebuffed slunk away to the bar, or their friends at their table.

They were about to call it a night when the batwing doors swung open, and a man entered. He was tall, broad shouldered, with a heavy black mustache and intense slate-grey eyes. He stopped just inside, looked around then walked to their table. As he approached, they noticed the glint of a badge from beneath his coat.

"Ladies," he said, stopping before them, "I'm Marshal Seth Bridges."

"Marshal," Roxy said.

"Would you mind tellin' me your names?"

"I'm Roxy Doyle."

"Liz Archer."

"May I sit for a moment?"

"You're the marshal," Roxy said.

Bridges sat with them.

"Can we buy you a drink?" Roxy asked

"No, thank you," the man said. "You ladies both have reputations."

"So?" Archer asked.

"I wonder what you're doin' here?"

"Marshal," Roxy said, "you knew we were here when you came in. I'm sure you've spoken with Mr. Turner, or Mr. Lewis, already."

"Or both," Archer said.

"That's true."

"Then you know why we're here."

"You think Mr. Lewis had somethin' to do with a price on Angel Eyes' head."

"That's right."

"What makes you believe so?" Bridges asked.

"The bounty is on your bank," Roxy said. "When I tried to collect it, the bank president, Turner, immediately went to Mr. Lewis' ranch."

"And you spoke to Mr. Lewis. He told you he wasn't involved."

"Correct."

"So why are you still here?"

"We're not convinced," Roxy said.

"What's your next move, then?"

"That's what we were sitting here trying to decide," Roxy told him.

"I have a suggestion," Bridges said.

"And what's that?"

Bridges raised his eyebrows

"I think you both should leave town."

Chapter Thirty-Three

"Are you ordering us out of town?" Roxy asked.

"I can't do that," Bridges said. "I have no valid reason. No, I'm suggestin' you leave town."

"Well," Archer said, "in that case, we refuse."

"Then I'll ask you not to start any trouble," the lawman said.

"We're not looking for trouble, Marshal," Archer said. "We're looking to avoid it. A couple of attempts have been made, already."

"On both of you?"

Roxy nodded.

"Are you partners, now?"

"Somebody mistook me for Liz, so we decided to join forces. I'm watching her back and she's watching mine, until we settle this thing."

"You're each very formidable on your own," Bridges said. "Together, I imagine you can be . . . explosive."

"Only to someone trying to kill us," Roxy said.

Bridges stood up. He appeared to be about six-foot-four.

"I hope that won't happen here," he said. "Goodnight, ladies."

As he walked away Archer said, "That's a good-lookin' man."

"You like older men?" Roxy asked.

"I like striking men," Archer said. "And very masculine ones. Age isn't so important to me."

"That's where we differ," Roxy said. "A man can be too young or too old."

"This marshal ain't too old."

"No," Roxy agreed, "he's not *too* old."

***

Roxy and Archer went to their hotel room, stripped down to underwear and climbed into their shared bed.

When Marshal Bridges got back to his office, Justin Turner was waiting there.

"Well?" he asked. "Are they leaving town?"

"No," Bridges said, seating himself behind his desk. "They're determined to stay and find out who put out that bounty."

"You were supposed to make them leave!" Turner said. "Order them to."

"I have no legal right to simply order them to leave town without a reason."

"I'll give you a reason," Turner said. "Mr. Lewis wants them gone."

"That may be a good enough reason for you, Mr. Turner, but not for the law."

"You know, Marshal," Turner said, "if you don't bend, some say you might break."

"If that's a threat, Mr. Turner, I wonder how you and your bank are going to enforce it."

"You're right, Bridges, I'm just a bank president," Turner said. "I was talking about the power a man like Mr. Lewis wields."

"You tell Mr. Lewis to come and see me about it," the lawman said. "If either of these ladies threatens him, I'll run them out of town."

"You might be held to that, Marshal," Turner said, and left.

Bridges took off his hat, tossed it onto the wall peg that he rarely missed, and sat back in his chair. He thought about Lady Gunsmith and Angel Eyes being in Millwood and thought there had never been two such beautiful ladies in town.

Beautiful and dangerous.

***

The next morning Roxy and Archer came down for breakfast and decided to find someplace other than the hotel to have it.

"There's a small place," Archer said, pointing. "Let's try that."

"Suits me."

They crossed the street and entered the little café. A waiter's eyes widened, and he hurriedly showed the two beauties to a table.

"What's good?" Archer asked him, smiling.

"C-c-corned beef hash and eggs," the young man stammered.

"We'll have that," Roxy said.

"Thanks, sweetie," Archer said to him.

"You got him all excited," Roxy said.

"Are you kidding? He's been staring at you."

"Just stop smiling at him and calling him sweetie," Roxy said.

"You're grumpy this morning," Archer said. "You need a man between your legs."

Roxy didn't argue that point. She had a dream about the foreman, Detmer, and indeed, woke up grumpy.

When the food came they discovered the waiter was right, the corned beef hash was delicious. And he seemed to have piled it up generously for them.

"I was hoping the marshal would come to our room last night," Archer admitted.

"And where did you think I'd sleep while you had your way with him?" Roxy asked.

"Oh, I was also hoping you'd go for a walk."

"Too bad neither of those things happened."

"I know," Archer said, "I could use a man, myself."

"I've been thinking maybe we should push things," Roxy said, "so we can leave this town and go our own ways."

"What do you have in mind?" Archer asked.

"I'm still working it out," Roxy said. "I'll tell you as soon as I think of a plan."

Chapter Thirty-Four

After they finished breakfast, they left the café and stopped just outside.

"Any ideas, yet?" Archer asked.

"I like your idea of scaring the bank president. Sticking a gun in his face."

"Was that my idea?"

Roxy shrugged.

"Yours or mine," she said.

"You think that'll get him to finger Lewis for us?"

"If not Lewis, then whoever it was that put the bounty on your head," Roxy said. "He'll just have to be convinced we'd kill him if he doesn't."

"I think we can do that," Archer said. "Or maybe we should just rob the bank."

"That would force the marshal to move against us," Roxy said. "We might end up killing him."

Archer made a face.

"I'd rather fuck him."

"So we won't rob the bank," Roxy said.

"Ah," Archer said, "we're not bank robbers. Then for sure there'd be a price on our heads."

"I had a talk with Turner when I got here," Roxy said. "Let's both try it and see what happens?"

Archer shrugged and said, "Let's go."

***

Five men faced one tall one in the back room of a saloon. They were all wearing gunbelts.

"You men know what's expected of you," the tall man said.

"It's pretty easy," one man said. "You want those two women dead."

"We want Angel Eyes dead," the tall man said. "If Roxy Doyle gets in the way, then her too. But the aim is to kill Liz Archer."

"And then get paid," another man said.

"And then collect the bounty," the tall man said. "After you kill 'er, go on over to the bank and see the president, Turner. He'll fork it over."

"Suits me," another said.

"We got to do it fair?" another asked.

"There are no rules about how you do it," the tall man said. "You want to bushwhack 'em, that's fine. As long as Archer ends up dead."

"What about the marshal?" the first man asked. "How's he gonna feel about it?"

"He can't say a thing about a fair fight," the tall man said. "And if they're bushwhacked, he can't prove who did it. That answer your question?"

All five men nodded.

"Then get out of here and pick your chance."

They all stood and left the back room. A couple of them stopped at the bar for a beer. The other three sat at a table and ordered whiskey.

***

Roxy and Liz entered the bank. Apparently, word had gotten out around town that they were there. The few customers in the bank hurried to leave. The two employees—a male teller and a female clerk—stared.

Roxy and Archer approached the teller's cage.

"We'd like to see Mr. Turner," Roxy said.

"I-I'll t-tell 'im you're here."

They waited while the teller went to Justin Turner's office. He returned in minutes.

"Mr. Turner will see you."

The two women walked into the office. Turner was standing behind his desk with his hands in plain sight.

"I have no gun," he said.

"We're not here to kill you, Turner," Roxy said. "This is Liz Archer. She wanted to meet you."

154

"Miss Archer, I'm pleased to mee—"

"Never mind the manners," Archer said. "You're holding the bounty money that's on my head. I want to know who you're holding it for."

"I can't talk about my depositors," Turner said.

"You better," Archer said. "If you don't, I'll be real unhappy."

"I know you're a famous gunhand," Turner said, "but like I told you, I'm unarmed. You're not going to shoot me in cold blood. Besides, that wouldn't answer your question."

"After you're dead," Roxy said, "we'll check your bank records. The name of whoever deposited that bounty has to be there."

"Now wait a minute," Turner said, suddenly nervous.

"We'll give you one last chance to tell us who it is," Archer said. "Or else we'll just kill you and look it up ourselves."

Chapter Thirty-Five

"I don't think you're going to do that," Marshal Seth Bridges said from behind them.

"Marshal!" Turner said, relieved. "You heard them threaten me. Lock them up!"

"I don't know that I'm going to lock them up," Bridges said, "but I'm going to walk them out of here. Come on, let's go, ladies."

Roxy turned and saw that the lawman's gun was still in his holster.

"We better go, Liz," Roxy said.

"I'm not finished with you, Mr. Turner," Archer said. "I suggest you talk to your depositor about removing that bounty from your bank."

Roxy and Archer turned, walked past the marshal and out of the bank. Marshal Bridges came out behind them and closed the bank door.

"What did you think you were up to?" he asked.

"How did you know we were up to anything?" Roxy asked.

"One of the customers you scared away came over to my office and told me something was up."

"We were just trying to get him to tell us who put the price on my head, Marshal."

"And then what?"

"And then we'd go see him and convince him to take it off," Archer said. "After all, I'm sure you don't want to see me killed in your town, do you?"

"I wouldn't want to see you killed anywhere, Miss Archer," Bridges said.

"That's very sweet of you."

"Then maybe," Roxy added, "you could convince Turner to give up the depositor's name."

"I could talk to him," Bridges said, "but I doubt it would do any good. Just like I don't think I could talk you ladies into leaving town."

"Not without what we came for," Archer said.

"What makes you think the answer's here?" the lawman asked.

"We suspected it when we rode in," Roxy said. "Now we're sure of it. After all, the bounty is definitely on deposit in your bank."

"And Randolph Lewis obviously told you about us," Archer said.

Marshal Bridges face grew red.

"I'm not in anybody's pocket," he growled, "least of all Randolph Lewis'."

157

"Sorry, Marshal," Archer said. "I didn't mean to insult you."

"Well, you did," Bridges said. "And if you cause any more trouble, I *will* be running you both out of town. Count on it!"

He turned and stormed away.

"I think you made him unhappy," Roxy said.

"I think you're right," Archer said. "I should probably apologize to him."

Before Roxy could respond, Archer started walking in the lawman's wake.

***

When Archer entered the marshal's office the man was in the act of tossing his hat onto the wall peg.

"Impressive," she said.

He looked at her from his desk.

"I haven't missed in twelve years," he said. "What insult did you forget to hit me with?"

"No insult." She closed the door. "I came to apologize."

"Apologize?" Bridges said, looking surprised.

"Sure," she said. "I apologize when I'm wrong."

"How often do you admit to being wrong?" he asked.

"Oh, not often."

"I didn't think so," he said. "Why this time?"

"I'm not sure," she said, "if it's those broad shoulders, or that mustache."

He stared at her for a few moments, then asked, "Coffee?"

"Sure."

"Have a seat."

She sat as he poured two cups of coffee and handed her one, then returned to his desk chair.

"I'm not sure," he said, "if this is some sort of joke, or tactic."

"Given the choice of those two," she said, "I'd say it was a tactic."

"Toward what?"

She sipped her coffee.

"Maybe toward you taking me into that cell block and removing all my clothes."

Now the lawman was surprised.

"We'd have to lock the door first, so nobody walks in on us."

"That'd make it more exciting," she said, "but if you insist, then by all means, lock the door."

As he got up to walk to the door and lock it, she rose and walked into the cellblock to wait.

Chapter Thirty-Six

When the marshal entered the cellblock, Archer was still fully dressed.

"Oh," he said, "you were serious."

"About you undressing me?" she asked. "Of course. I'm not going to make it easy for you."

But she had taken off her hat and tossed it aside, so that her blonde hair hung to her shoulders.

"Why don't we start with this?" he asked, undoing her gunbelt.

"Just don't put it too far away," she said, as he set it aside with his own.

"We're in jail, Miss Archer," he said. "You couldn't be safer."

"It's just a habit I don't like to break," she said. "It's why I'm still alive."

"I'm glad you are."

He approached her and started to unbutton her shirt.

"You have a gentle touch for a big man," Archer commented.

"Is that good?" he asked.

"For now, very good."

***

After Archer headed for Bridges' office, two of the five gunmen were walking across the street from the hotel and spotted Roxy in front.

"Look," one said, "the redhead."

"We could get the others and take her now," the second man said.

"The blonde is the one with the price on her head," the first man reminded him. "She's the priority."

"Yeah, but we might as well take advantage of the chance to get rid of this one," the second man said. "Then the blonde would be meat."

"Okay," the first one said, "but hurry and bring 'em back before we lose—wait!"

The second man had taken two steps and stopped.

"What?"

"Look."

They both saw the foreman of the Lewis ranch riding down the street.

"Forget it," the first man said. "We'll take 'em when we see 'em together."

They watched as the foreman reigned in his horse in front of the redhead.

***

Roxy sat in front of the hotel for a short while, then thought about going back to her room. In the act of standing, she saw the foreman, Kyle Detmer, riding into town. As she watched he rode toward her, stopped and dismounted. He was almost as tall as Marshal Bridges, but some ten or fifteen years younger.

"Mr. Detmer," she said. "What brings you to town?"

"Kyle," he said, "just call me Kyle."

"Kyle," she said, "what's on your mind?"

"Can we talk?"

"About what?" she asked. "Your boss?"

"Yes," Kyle said, "but I'd like to talk in private."

"The hotel bar?"

"How about your room?"

That surprised her.

"Unless you're afraid to have a man in your room," he added.

She gave him a look and said, "Follow me."

She led him into the hotel lobby and up to the room she shared with Archer.

Detmer looked around at the two sets of saddlebags, the two beds that had been slept in.

"You two are sharin' a room?" he asked.

"That's right," Roxy said. "So what's this about?"

"My boss insists he has nothin' to do with the bounty on Archer's head."

162

"And you believe him?"

"I don't know," he said. "I've stood next to him while he lied to people, but that was business. I've never known him to lie for personal reasons."

"Do you still work for him? Did you quit? Or did he fire you for questioning him?"

"I still work for him."

"Did he send you to talk to me?"

"No," Detmer said, "he doesn't know I'm here."

"Then why are you here?"

"To tell you the truth, I'm not sure," he said. "Maybe because I want to help you and Miss Archer. Or maybe it's because I've never kissed a woman wearin' a gun."

That surprised Roxy. She didn't think the foreman was capable of being that charming. She thought he was simply a cowhand. A handsome cowhand.

"Well," she said, "why don't you go ahead?"

***

Across the street, in a jail cell, Marshal Bridges and Liz Archer peeled each other's clothes off until they were both completely naked.

Archer was impressed with the physique of the man, who seemed robust, without an ounce of fat, although he had to be in his late 40s. His cock was large and growing larger by the moment.

When Bridges peeled off the last of Archer's clothes he stood back and stared, transfixed by her beauty. Her full breasts were tipped with pink nipples, most of her skin was pale, except for her hands, neck and face, which had been tanned by constant exposure to the sun.

Archer could wait no longer. She ran her hands over his body, until she was holding his rigid cock in both hands, stroking it. She fell to her knees, rubbed the hot column of flesh over her cheeks and then opened her mouth and took it inside. She sucked it until it was glistening with her saliva, and then allowed him to lift her to her feet, encircle her in his arms, and kiss her . . .

***

Detmer took Roxy in his arms and kissed her. She returned the kiss with a hot fervor, and when their mouth's parted, she asked, "So, how is it kissing a woman wearing a gun?"

"Excitin'," he said. "But I think I'd like us to try it without the gun."

"So then do it again, you fool!" she said, lifting her face to his.

Chapter Thirty-Seven

When Kyle Detmer removed Roxy's gunbelt and set it down very near—at her insistence—he did not stop there. He continued to remove her garments until she was fully naked. He caught his breath when he saw her full, brown-tipped breasts, and stood transfixed.

"Well," she said, "if you're just going to stand there, I suppose I should take off your clothes."

He wasn't wearing a gun, so she started with his boots, then yanked down his trousers and underwear. When his hard cock sprang into view, she was nose to tip with it. Laughing, she used her tongue to wet the tip, then continued til she had him naked, as well.

Once his clothes were gone, Detmer sprang into action, running his hands over her body. She moaned as he took her nipples between his thumb and forefinger and squeezed them, then slid his hands beneath her full breasts and lifted them to his mouth. He sucked and bit her nipples until she squealed, then pushed her down on the bed and onto her back. She spread her legs as an invitation for him to do whatever he wanted. She was just pleased that she was finally going to exorcise her sexual frustration . . .

***

Archer and Bridges tried using the cot in the cell first, with her on her back and him atop her. But there was no room for the two of them, and the cot threatened to break.

"Here," she said, "let's try this."

She went to the bars, climbed up on them, her bare feet in the slots used to slide food trays to prisoners, and lifted her butt for him. That gorgeous bottom of hers was just at the right height. He stepped close to her, gripped her hips and slid his long cock into her wet pussy from behind. She began to bounce up and down on his hot penis.

They continued like that for a good long while, Archer enjoying the sensation of his smooth cock gliding in and out of her, until she began to feel the strain in her legs.

"Uh-oh," she gasped, as the strength went from her arms and legs at the same time. But he didn't allow her to fall. He simply put his arms beneath her thighs and held her, so he could continue to plumb her depths. A strong man, he kept her bouncing for some time more before he lifted her from his cock, tossed her in the air, reversing her in his arms, and then impaling her once again.

This time as he bounced her up and down on his root, she wrapped her arms around his neck and held on for dear life. Finally, she felt his body go rigid, and then he was exploding inside her with a roar . . .

***

In the hotel room across the street, Detmer was lying atop Roxy, driving his hard cock in and out of her while she kept her legs spread.

Abruptly, he withdrew, balanced himself on his arms and looked down at her lovely face. Both their bodies were beaded with sweat, and to him it only increased her beauty.

"If you don't mind," he said, "I want to taste you."

"You mean . . . my pussy?"

"That's what I mean."

She smiled up at him.

"Please," she said, "taste all you want."

He slid down her body, kissing his way from her neck, breasts and belly, enjoying the salt of her sweat along the way. When he reached her hot, wet pussy, he put his mouth and tongue to work, apparently knowing exactly what he was doing.

"Oh, God," she said, "you've done this before."

"Once or twice," he admitted.

"With whores, I suppose?"

He looked up at her, his face now gleaming with her running juice.

"Once or twice," he said again, and bent to resume his task, which seemed to be to give her as much pleasure as he could.

She spread her legs even wider for him, and he put his hands to work, as well. He slid two fingers in and out of her hot depths, as he continued to lick and suck on her. Waves of pleasure coursed through her body several times over until, the fourth time, she actually let out a muffled scream . . .

***

"I'd like to return the favor," she said to him, breathlessly.

"Please do," he said, lying down on his back.

She kissed him, then worked her way down over his torso and belly until she was once again nose to tip with his large cock. She took time to lick the length of him, wetting him thoroughly, before gliding his penis into her mouth, taking as much of the length as she could. She then began to suck him avidly, bobbing her head up and down, until she felt his legs quiver, and he exploded into her mouth . . .

Chapter Thirty-Eight

The cot in the jail cell was sturdy enough to hold the marshal's weight, as he sat on it, allowing Archer to kneel between his legs and suck him until he once again exploded . . .

***

The cot also allowed them to sit side-by-side, so they could both catch their breath. They each sat with their elbows on their knees, since the wall behind them was filthy.

"To tell you the truth," Bridges said, "I never expected this."

"I did," Archer said.

"I would've thought I was a little old for you," he admitted.

"You don't think you're old," she said.

"But I thought a woman like you would think so."

"A woman like me?"

"Young, beautiful, vibrant."

"I like real men, Marshal," she said. "You're a real man."

"And you're quite a woman." He stood up. "We better get dressed, I have to unlock the office."

They dressed and left the cellblock. Marshal Bridges unlocked the door.

"That was a foolish thing for me to do, but I couldn't resist."

"Neither could I. Can we heat up this coffee?"

"Sure."

He took the mug from her, poured it back into the pot, then poured a new mug full.

"Tell me, what are you and Miss Doyle planning to do?" Bridges asked.

"We haven't decided yet," Archer said. "But I know we're not leaving town until we get this bounty off my head."

"And how do you plan to do that? Kill the guilty party?"

"That's up to him—or her—when we find them."

"You think it might be a woman?"

"Could be a woman, could be because of a woman."

"Have you killed many women?" he asked.

"I've never killed a woman . . . ever."

"Then this bounty might be because of a man you killed."

"There've been a lot of those," she told him. "How do I decide which one?"

"By sticking a gun in Mr. Turner's face?"

"Not quite," Archer said. "We were just asking him again, this time together."

"Thinking you'd scare him?"

"Hoping, I guess." She finished her coffee and stood up. "I hope to see you again, Marshal—on good terms."

"Don't cause any trouble, Miss Archer," he said, "and we will."

She tossed him a smile and left.

***

Roxy and Detmer dressed and went downstairs for a drink.

"I need your help, Kyle. We've got to find out if Mr. Lewis is behind this bounty. And if he is, why."

"Maybe I can find something out," Detmer said. "Don't do anything foolish until we see if I can."

"Okay, thanks."

"No," he said, with a cocky grin, "thank you."

He headed out the batwing doors, passing Archer along the way.

"That man's got a big smile on his face," Archer said, joining Roxy at the table. "Does it mean what I think it means?"

"It means he's going to try and help us," Roxy said.

"He is? How?"

"By finding out if his boss is really behind this mess," Roxy said, "and why."

"The marshal gave me an idea," Archer said.

"He did?" Roxy asked. "You mean, you had time to talk?"

"A little," she said. "He understands we can't leave, but he doesn't want trouble."

"Seems to me it's going to go one way or the other," Roxy said. "Either we leave town, or there's going to be trouble a-plenty."

"If we've got the patience, and Lewis really is the man we're looking for, I'm thinking we may just have to wait."

"That may be the case whether he's the man or not."

"But if not him, then who?"

"I don't know," Roxy said, "but the money's in his bank, so this has to be the place for us to find out."

"So we're back where we started," Archer said. "Push or sit back and wait. I'll get us two more beers."

Archer collected the beers from the bar and came back.

"You look more relaxed," she said, setting one mug in front of Roxy. "That foreman knew his way around your lady parts?"

"He did that," Roxy said. "And the marshal? Turns out he's not so old?"

"Just old enough," Archer said, and they laughed and clinked glasses.

Chapter Thirty-Nine

Across the street from the saloon five men gathered. One of them had seen Roxy and Detmer enter the saloon. He had run to gather the other four men from another saloon, and when they reached this one, the Ten of Clubs, they saw Liz Archer going in, and the foreman, Detmer, coming out.

"Okay," one man said, "we've got them both in the same place, and he's out of the way."

"Should we go in and get 'em?" another man asked.

"No," the first man said. "Let's take 'em on the outside. There'll be less chance some hero will try to help 'em."

"Okay," a third man said, "as soon as they come through those doors, we open fire."

"Right," the first man said. "We fill 'em with as much lead as we can."

"And then we claim the bounty," another said.

"Exactly," the first man replied. "But let's get set up."

They put their heads together and came up with their places.

And waited.

***

Roxy and Archer had decided to have one more drink and then retire to their hotel.

"Unless you and the foreman tore up the room," Archer added.

"No, we confined ourselves to my bed. What did you and the marshal do to his office? Did his desk stand up to the weight?"

Archer smiled.

"We confined ourselves to a jail cell."

Roxy looked surprised.

"How did that work?" she asked. "No, never mind. I'll do without the details. I'll get the drinks."

Roxy rose and walked to the bar. On the way she glanced out the large front window. She got the two beers and took them back to the table. As Archer reached for one, she stopped her.

"Don't drink it."

"Why not?"

"We've got company out front," Roxy said. "We need to be sharp."

"Who's out there?"

"Looks like three, maybe more. Right across the street. They're probably planning on opening fire as soon as we step out."

"So we step out the back."

"One of us does," Roxy said. "The other one goes out the front."

"Why?"

"To confuse them."

"How so?"

"They'll wonder why only one of us is coming out," Roxy said. "Where's the other one?"

"And that gives one of us time to get set."

"Right."

"So which one of us goes out the front?"

"Me."

"Why you?"

"Because the bounty's on your head. They're liable to start shooting as soon as they see you."

"And what if they shoot as soon as they see you?"

"They won't."

"Roxy, you've been mistaken for me before."

"I'll keep my hat in my hand, so they can see my red hair clearly."

"You're taking a big chance.

"You go out the back, work your way along the alley to the front, see how many there are."

"Then what?"

"Then we'll both step into the street, far enough apart that we'll split their attention."

"And then we take them."

"Only we try to keep at least one of them alive, so we can talk."

"Sounds okay to me."

"There's one more thing."

"What's that?"

"When we both step into the street," Roxy said, "they might all shoot at you, first."

"We'll have to take that chance," Archer said. "They might all shoot at you when you step through the doors. We're both taking a chance, Roxy."

"Okay," Roxy said, "as long as we both know that."

"Give me five minutes and then step out," Archer said. "I'll be in place by then."

"You better be."

Archer smiled and ran to the bar.

"Is there a back room?" she asked the bartender.

"A storeroom," the man said. "Go through this door behind the bar."

"Thanks."

She ran through the door and stopped short. There was no back door.

Chapter Forty

Roxy made her way to the batwing doors and tried to peer out without being seen. She gave it what she felt was five minutes and, believing Archer was in position, she stepped through the doors . . .

***

The five men across the street were spread out, but all had their eyes on the batwing doors. When they opened, they almost went for their guns, and then saw that only one woman was stepping out. It was not the blonde, Angel Eyes, but the redhead. They all exchanged a glance, and the first man indicated they should all wait . . .

***

Archer panicked for only a moment, then ran to the only window. Because of past thefts, the window was nailed shut. She looked around, found a two-by-four, and used it to smash the window. She continued to use the piece of wood to clear the shards, then climbed out and hurried along the ally to the street. She peeked out and saw five men positioned across the street, spread out. She hoped they didn't start firing as soon as Roxy stepped out . . .

***

Roxy stepped through the doors, stopped just outside, removing her hat, revealing her incredible red hair. She didn't know how anyone had ever mistaken her for Liz Archer, but removing her hat hopefully made sure it didn't happen again.

This time, anyway . . .

***

One man ran to the first, the self-appointed leader of the group

"What do we do?" he asked.

"We wait," the first man said. "We want the blonde, or both of them, but not the redhead alone. Nobody fires a shot until I do. Pass that along . . ."

The second man ran back to the other three, one-by-one, and told them not to fire until the first man did.

"What makes him the boss?" one man questioned.

"He did," the second man said, "and I didn't hear anyone else steppin' up."

The second man went back to his place . . .

***

The self-appointed leader of the group spotted Angel Eyes stepping out of the alley next to the Ten of Clubs Saloon. Frantically, he waved to the other men . . .

***

Roxy put her hat back on and stepped into the street. She saw the one man frantically waving at the others, then saw why. She glanced to her right and watched Liz Archer stepping from the alley.

All five men drew their guns, and Roxy followed their example.

When the firing started, it was difficult to see who was actually firing at who.

Roxy began to fire, and dove for the cover of a nearby horse trough . . .

Chapter Forty-One

Archer came out of the alley, her heart pounding. She didn't want Roxy to get killed because of her. The first shot struck the building behind her, telling her that they were not only firing at Roxy. She drew her gun and began shooting.

***

The five gunmen ducked for cover. This was not turning out as they had planned. The two women were supposed to be easy pickings as they left the saloon. Instead, they had come out apart separately.

"Damn!" the first man swore. "Start shootin'!"

***

Archer sought cover as hot lead started flying around her. She returned fire, but the five gunmen scattered when the two ladies returned their fire.

Two of the gunmen stood their ground, exchanged lead with Roxy and Archer and, as a result, quickly ate dirt and ended up dead.

The other three panicked and ran.

Roxy and Archer got to their feet and each pointed which way they were going. They were still, determined to take one man alive.

While people on the street scattered and ducked for cover, Roxy ran to the left, and Archer to the right. As it turned out, that left Roxy pursuing two gunmen, while Archer ran after one.

***

Roxy chased her two attackers down the street. They were throwing shots back at her while more citizens ducked and fled. She wanted at least one of them alive, but as they split up, she fired and caught one high in the back. The other one had gone right, and as the first one fell, Roxy followed.

She held her fire this time as he cut down an alley.

***

Liz Archer pursued her man up the street, aware that there were locals running in the street between them to get out of the way of the flying bullets. Archer knew she could put a hunk of lead right in the man's back, but there was always the chance someone would suddenly run between them and catch it. That had happened to a man she knew, Lancaster, who had killed a child. It took him lots of years and whiskey to recover from it.

When the man turned a corner, however, they were suddenly on a deserted street.

"Stop right there!" she shouted. "I don't want to kill you, but I will."

She saw the man hesitate and stumble, and at that point he had no choice but to turn and face her, gun in hand. She stopped and they stared at each other.

***

Roxy followed her man down an alley. When she came out the other side, she saw that the gunman had run into a group of children playing there, and had grabbed one. Now he turned to face her, holding a nine or ten-year-old boy in front of him. She stopped running.

"Back off, or I'll kill this kid!" he shouted.

"You're a fool," she said to him. "You should have picked a bigger kid."

There was plenty of his chest available to her, so she fired and put a bullet just above the boy's head. As the man released him, the boy fled, which was fine with Roxy. She had a feeling she might have given him a bit of a haircut.

183

The gunman's weapon slipped from his hand, and he slumped to the ground, dead.

She turned to run back the way she came, hoping Archer had better luck and taken her man alive.

***

Archer could see the man's mind racing, trying to figure if he had a chance. She decided to play on her name in an attempt to take him alive.

"Come on," she said. "You know who I am. You might've had a chance with your friends. Five to one was good odds, but one-to-one you're dead."

The man's face was covered with sweat and his eyes were wild. She hoped he was going to make the right choice, and she wouldn't have to take the chance of wounding him and hope he didn't get off a good shot.

When you shot to wound, you always took the chance of getting killed.

Chapter Forty-Two

As Roxy got back to the Ten of Clubs Saloon, she saw Archer coming from the other direction, leading a man who was holding his shoulder, blood leaking from between his fingers. Also standing in front of the saloon was Marshal Bridges, watching both women. Inside the saloon customers were staring out the windows, and from above the batwing doors.

Roxy reached the lawman first and he said, "I see Miss Archer got hers alive."

"Yeah, sorry," Roxy said. "My two wouldn't give up."

"Looks like she didn't give hers a choice," he said. "She winged him."

"She must be a better shot than I am," Roxy said. She figured Archer had taken a chance of wounding the man to take him alive. It was a foolish thing to do, but she got away with it.

As Archer reached them, Roxy asked, "Did he talk?"

"Not yet." She looked at the marshal. "We need a doc."

"Follow me."

He led the two women and the wounded man down the street and stopped in front of a shingle that read: JOHN OLIVE, M.D.

He stepped to the door and banged his fist on it. A harried looking man in his fifties opened it and glared.

"I was takin' a nap," he complained. "I was up all night deliverin' a stubborn baby."

"Well, I got a customer for you, Doc."

He looked past the lawman at the two women with the bleeding man between them.

"Bring him in."

They got the man into the office, and the doctor took him into his examination room, leaving the three of them in the waiting area.

"I guess this is as good a time as any for an explanation," Marshal Bridges said.

"It's easy," Archer said. "Five of them were waiting for us outside the saloon. Four of them are dead, and the fifth one is in there."

"Well," the lawman said, "I heard all the shooting, so I guess you were defending yourselves."

"You better believe it!" Roxy snapped. "You shouldn't even be questioning us."

"I'm doing my job, Miss Doyle."

"A little late to the party, if you ask me."

"Easy, Roxy," Archer said. "We got one. Let's see what he has to say."

"You're the one they were after," Roxy said. "You should be pissed!"

Bridges looked at Archer, who simply shrugged.

"Well, you ladies can wait to talk to your man," he said. "If you need anything I'll be in my office."

"Thanks, Marshal," Archer said.

After the lawman left, Roxy looked at Archer and said, "Thanks? I assume that was for your time in his cell, because he was no help just now."

"It all happened so fast, we were gone by the time he got there."

"You can make excuses—" Roxy started but stopped when the doctor appeared.

"He's gonna be fine," he said, drying his hand on a towel. "I got the bullet out."

"We need to talk to him," Archer said.

"He needs to rest—"

"Now!" Roxy snapped.

"Yeah, okay," the doctor said. "Go on in."

Roxy and Archer entered the room. The man was lying flat on his back, with a bandaged shoulder. He turned his head to look at them and his eyes widened.

"This wasn't my idea!" He hurriedly blurted.

"We know that," Archer said. Roxy had decided to allow Archer to do the talking. "We want to know whose idea it was."

"I don't know," he said, "I swear."

"But you know who recruited you for the job," Archer said.

"Yah, his name was Bates," the man said. "He said we was gonna get easy money."

"I find that insulting," Roxy said.

"What's your name, friend?" Archer asked.

"Uh, I'm Buzzard."

"What's your whole name?"

"I'm just called Buzzard. People have always said when they look at me, they see a buzzard."

Archer figured that had something to do with the arch in the man's long neck.

"Okay, Buzzard," she said. "Bates recruited you for what was supposed to be an easy pay day. But who was it who put up the money?"

"Dunno, I swear," Buzzard said. "I just know Bates was signing men up."

Archer was willing to accept keeping this man alive to be a lost cause.

"Come on," she said, "Bates must've told you who recruited him."

"Well . . . yeah," Buzzard said, "but you ain't gonna believe it."

Archer exchanged a glance with Roxy, and then said, "Try us."

Chapter Forty-Three

Roxy and Archer left the doctor's office. Roxy knew Archer was conflicted. At least, she thought she was. As it turned out, Archer was angry.

"That sonofabitch!" she seethed.

"I was wondering why he left so hastily," Roxy said. "I thought he'd want to put Buzzard in a cell. After all, he and his friends were shooting up the streets."

"What I don't understand is," Archer said, "he had me in one of his cells. He could've killed me himself."

"He might be the kind of lawman who doesn't mind being someone's bag man," Roxy proposed, "but not a killer."

"Well," Archer said, "he's the one who can confirm that Lewis is the man who put that price on my head. We just have to make him talk."

"Wait," Roxy said, "We have to play this smart."

"How so?"

"Let's not tell him we know he's involved," Roxy said.

"So what *do* you want to tell him?"

"How's this?" Roxy asked . . .

***

"I didn't expect to see you two again so soon," the marshal said, as they entered his office.

"Well, we got the man to talk," Roxy said.

"Oh?"

"His name's Buzzard," Archer said, "and he said he was working for Mr. Lewis."

"He said that?" Bridges looked surprised.

"He did," Roxy said. "We're going to ride out there and confront the man. And since he's a big important rancher, we thought we should bring the law with us."

"I know Buzzard," Bridges said. "I'm surprised he talked."

"He's still at the doc's," Roxy said, "if you want to bring him in and put him in a cell."

"After all," Archer said," he did try to gun us down on the street."

"Oh, yeah, right," the lawman said. "I'll do that. Uh, when do you want to ride out to Mr. Lewis' ranch?"

"There's no hurry," Archer said. "We can do it to-morrow."

"Okay, fine," he said. "I'll meet you both in front of the hotel at nine a.m."

"That's fine, Marshal," Roxy said. "Thanks."

"No problem," he said, "it's my job."

Both women nodded and left.

Just outside the office Roxy said, "Okay, let's see how fast he rides out to see Lewis."

"With us on his tail," Archer added.

They moved across the street. In front of the hardware store they secreted themselves behind some crates.

***

Sometime later Roxy and Archer rode out of town after the marshal.

"I give him credit," Roxy said. "He locked Buzzard up first."

"At least he did that part of his job," Archer said.

"So now he's got to warn Randolph Lewis we're coming because his latest group of gunmen didn't get the job done," Roxy said.

"Buzzard must have denied telling us he worked for Lewis," Archer said. "Think the marshal believed him?"

"I bet not," Roxy said. "That's probably why he left him in jail."

They trailed Marshal Bridges all the way to the ranch, staying far enough behind him to go unseen.

"By the time we head back to town, it's going to be dark," Roxy said. "Not much chance of anyone trying to bushwhack us at night."

"We'll have to see about that after we confront both Lewis and Bridges," Archer said. "They're not going to be very happy with us. We may have to shoot our way off the ranch."

"That's probably going to be the case," Roxy said, "if he's got more gunmen out there besides ranch hands."

"It would be nice if we got an answer to our question," Archer said. "Just why does Randolph Lewis want me dead bad enough to put up a bounty?"

"What do you say we don't leave without an answer?" Roxy proposed.

"That sounds good to me."

***

By the time Roxy and Archer reached the ranch, Marshal Bridges had already gone inside the house. His horse was still out front.

They stopped by the barn to look the grounds over.

"The hands must be out at work," Roxy said.

"Unless there's a gun behind every bush."

"I guess there's one way to find out."

They rode their horses up to the house and stopped alongside the lawman's animal. They looked around before dismounting, didn't see anyone nearby.

"This place is too quiet," Archer said.

"The marshal hasn't been here long enough for them to hide their men," Roxy said. "I think they're out mending fences or rounding up stock."

"Suits me either way," Archer said. "Let's go inside."

They approached the front door.

Chapter Forty-Four

They were surprised that the door was opened by Lewis, himself.

"Ladies," the man said. "I've been expecting you. Come in."

"So you're ready to tell the truth?" Archer asked.

"Indeed," he said. "Please, come in and follow me."

He led them to a room in the back of the house. The walls were lined with books. There were two leather chairs, a small desk, and a sideboard with various liquor bottles on it.

"Can I offer you a drink?"

"No thanks," Roxy said. "We're not here to drink."

"Are you here to kill me?"

"We're here to get some answers," Archer said. "What happens after that is up to you."

"I see." The man didn't seem the least bit nervous. "I heard you put on quite a show in town today."

"We defended ourselves, if that's what you mean," Roxy said.

"Yes, that is what I heard." He sat down behind the small desk. "Please, have a seat."

"That's okay," Roxy said. "We'll stand."

"We're quite alone in the house," Lewis said. "And my hands are out in the field."

"So where's the marshal?" Archer asked.

"Oh, he led you here, and then went out the back door," Lewis said. "There was another horse waiting for him there. By now he's on his way back to town."

Roxy and Archer exchanged a glance.

"Oh, you thought he didn't know you were tailing him? He's quite good at his job."

"He had his chance to kill me," Archer said, "and he didn't."

"The marshal is a good lawman, not a killer," Lewis said.

"Then why did he rush out here to warn you we were coming?" Roxy asked.

"He's also a good friend."

"All right, never mind that," Archer said. "Why the hell did you put a bounty out on my head?"

"That's easy," Lewis said, sitting back in his chair. "I hate your guts."

"Why?" Roxy asked. "Why would you hate her enough to pay to have her killed?"

"I'm dying," he said. "My doctor says it's a matter of months."

"Why is that my fault?" Archer asked.

"It's not," he said. "You come under the heading of unfinished business, for me."

"That's not an explanation," Roxy said.

"No, it's not," he said. "Do you remember a boy named Daniel Lewis?"

"A boy?" Archer asked.

"A young man," Lewis said. "It was about ten years ago."

Archer thought a moment, then shook her head.

"I don't remember."

"You wouldn't," Lewis said. "He was . . . unremarkable. But he was my son."

"And?" Roxy asked.

"And after he met her," Lewis said, "and she left him behind, he was depressed, and . . . he killed himself." He looked at Archer. "Because he loved you, and you left."

"I may not remember him," Archer said, "but I've never told any man I loved him."

"That doesn't matter," Lewis said. "He killed himself because of you."

"How do you know that?" Roxy asked.

"He left a note. I still have it." He opened his desk drawer, took a piece of paper out and handed it to Archer.

"She doesn't love me. She's gone. I don't want to live without her. I'm sorry."

She handed the note to Roxy.

"This doesn't say he's talking about Liz," Roxy said, handing it back.

"He was," Lewis said, putting the note back in the drawer. "I'm sure of it."

"But why go after her all these years later?" Roxy asked.

"I told you," he said. "I'm dying, and this is unfinished business. So if you want to kill another member of the Lewis family, go ahead."

Archer came around the desk and crouched down in front of the man. When she spoke, it was in a soft, kind voice.

"I don't want to kill anyone," Archer said. "But if you keep that bounty on my head, I'll have to, again and again, to protect myself. You'll be responsible for many deaths."

"It would make more sense for you to remove the bounty," Roxy added. "Keep anyone else from being killed."

"My son—"

"Your son was weak," Roxy said. "Whether it was Liz or another woman he was talking about, there were other ways to go. He didn't have to kill himself. He took the easy way out. I get the feeling his father's never done that."

"No," Lewis said, "no, I haven't. I've always fought for what I got."

"Well," Roxy said, "it's too bad your son didn't feel that way. He left his daughter alone, and you're doing the same thing."

"What do you—"

"Rather than waste the next few months of your life causing the deaths of many men, why not use that time to find someone who will take care of Lisa when you're gone?"

"She'll need someone," Archer said. "Someone to care for her and guide her. It's going to be a difficult time for her."

"So, you're not going to kill me?" he asked.

"That's up to Liz," Roxy said.

Lewis looked at Archer.

"I told you," she said. "I don't want to kill anyone. I'm going to leave it up to you." She looked at Roxy. "Let's go."

Chapter Forty-Five

Roxy and Archer went back to their horses and headed back to town as dusk fell.

"Do you buy that story? Roxy asked. "About his son?"

"About his son taking his own life? I'm not sure he did it because of me. I don't usually waste my time with weak men, and I'm usually a good judge."

Roxy didn't respond.

"I know what you're thinking," Archer said. "Bridges may be bent, but he's not weak."

"I'd have to agree, there," Roxy said. "How do you want to handle him? Alone?"

"Not really," Archer said. "I might just put a bullet in him."

"He's wearing a badge," Roxy reminded her.

"I know. Maybe if you're with me, I won't do it."

"Hey," Roxy said, "if you want me to put a bullet in him, I will."

"Why don't we see what he has to say for himself?" Archer suggested.

"Fine. As soon as we get back. Let's not give him time to think."

"He's a man," Archer said. "How much thinking can he do?

I've learned that men are good for one thing. I use them for that and move on."

Suddenly, Roxy thought Archer might just have been the reason Randolph Lewis' son killed himself. And she wondered if she had ever affected a man that way? After all, her opinion of men was much the same.

***

"Ladies," Bridges said, when they entered his office. "I thought we were meeting in the morning?"

"That was before we all rode out to the Lewis ranch," Archer said.

He grinned.

"Did you think I wouldn't see you following me?"

"We thought you wouldn't care."

"Would you like to sit?"

"We'll stand," Archer said.

"Suit yourselves." The lawman leaned back in his chair, affording himself an easier draw if it came to that. "What did he have to say?"

"He admitted to placing the bounty on my head," Archer said.

"Did he, now?"

"He said you were being helpful because you're friends," Roxy said.

"He's right," Bridges said, "we are friends."

"So close that you'd hire gunmen to shoot us down in the street?" Roxy asked.

"That wasn't personal," he answered.

"You fingered us to be killed," Archer said. "You fingered me after we had sex. I take that personal."

"I doubt you ever took sex that personal," the lawman said. "We used each other. That was it. Lewis and me, we've been friends a long time."

"Do you believe his reason for putting a price on my head?" Archer asked.

"Which one, his son killing himself, or him being ill? Yeah, I believe both. Why wouldn't I?"

"And the banker, Turner?" Archer said. "What's his part?"

"He's just holding the money, waiting to pay it out. You've got no reason to kill him."

"Are you saying we have reason to kill you?" Archer asked.

"Rather than a banker or a dying man? Yeah, I guess I'd be elected."

"If we wanted to kill somebody," Roxy said.

"Which we don't."

"You can relax, Marshal," Archer said. "You're not going to need to skin that hogleg."

He relaxed his hand.

"If I did, either one of you could probably outdraw me," he said. "What do you intend to do now?"

"We think Lewis will be removing the bounty," Archer said. "That's all we wanted when we came here."

"You can check with Turner in the morning," Bridges said.

"We'll do that," Roxy said.

They both turned to go to the door.

"What about Buzzard?" the lawman asked. "What do you want me to do with him?"

"For all we care you can let him out," Archer said. "I don't think he'll be coming after us again."

"Not even if the bounty's still there," Bridges agreed. "I'll let him go in the morning."

"If the bounty is lifted, we'll be gone tomorrow, as well," Roxy said.

Bridges looked at Archer.

"Don't we get to say a proper goodbye?"

She shook her head. "Not a chance."

***

On the way to the hotel Roxy asked Archer, "So you think it's over?"

"I think you got to him," Archer said. "But we'll know more when we talk to the banker tomorrow."

"And what about the marshal?"

"He knows his limitations. I don't think we have to worry about him."

They reached the hotel, looked both ways on the street, and went into the lobby.

"What are you going to do after this?" Archer asked.

"What I was doing before," Roxy said. "Look for my father."

"I hope you find him," Archer said, "but . . . be very careful."

"Of what?"

"Of what you might find."

They reached the room and went inside.

"That's just it," Roxy said, sitting on her bed. "I don't know what to expect."

"My advice is," Archer said, sitting on hers, "be ready for anything."

Chapter Forty-Six

In the morning, after breakfast, they went to the bank together. Along the way they didn't pass anyone.

"It's too quiet," Roxy said.

"Yeah, it is," Archer said. "Maybe we misread Lewis."

"Or maybe he simply hasn't removed the bounty yet," Roxy said. "People are still expecting trouble."

"Let's get this over with," Archer said.

They entered the bank, found it empty. They went to Turner's door and knocked.

"Come!"

They opened the door and went in, one at a time, to cover each other front and back. Turner was seated behind his desk.

"Come in, Ladies," he said.

They closed the door behind them.

"Have you heard from Mr. Lewis this morning?" Archer asked.

"No," Turner said, "what was I supposed to hear?"

"To remove the bounty."

Turner sat back.

"Really? I haven't heard that."

"You will," Roxy said.

"Maybe," Turner said, standing. "Why don't you come with me? I want to show you something."

He walked to the door, opened it and left the office. They followed. He took them to the front of the bank and pointed.

"Look."

They looked out the window at what had been an empty street. Now there was at least a dozen armed men out there, waiting.

"You can't go out the back," he said. "That's covered, too."

"Have you spoken to the marshal this morning?" Roxy asked.

"I have, yes."

They looked at each other, and then at him.

"This is wrong," Roxy said.

"This has to be over," Turner said. "Mr. Lewis needs this, before he dies."

"Who are these men?" Roxy asked.

"Just guns for hire," Turner said. "None of them can stand up to you alone, but all of them . . ." He trailed off and shrugged.

"You're a banker," Roxy said, "not the leader of a gang of gunmen."

"Let Roxy go," Archer said, "and I'll walk out there."

"I can't do that," Turner said. "She might come back to take revenge for you."

"I might, at that," Roxy said.

"So what do you suggest?" Archer asked Roxy.

"Well," Roxy said, "we could take Mr. Turner out there with us."

"Good luck with that," Turner said. "Those men don't care a lick about me."

Roxy and Archer looked at each other.

"Could we have read Lewis wrong, last night?" Roxy asked.

"I guess we did."

They both looked at Turner.

"Ladies, I'm sorry," he said. "I'm just the banker."

"And if we kill you," Roxy said, "they still get paid, right?"

"Right," Turner said. "Whoever takes my place will pay the money out."

"They're all going to have to split the money," Archer said.

"Look at them," Roxy said. "They're all fifty-dollar guns."

"I'd hate for my epitaph to say 'Killed by fifty dollar guns!' " Archer said.

"Well," Roxy said, "there's no point in putting it off."

Turner backed away so he wouldn't be struck by errant lead or flying glass.

Roxy put her hand on the door, and suddenly a rider appeared, riding hell-bent-for-leather, right into the middle of the street, waving his arms frantically. Behind him came a man in a buggy, who also stopped between the gunmen and the bank.

Turner moved forward, peered out the window and said, "Mr. Lewis."

***

The foreman, Kyle Detmer, entered the bank and looked at the two ladies.

"You're free and clear," he said, then looked at Turner. "Mr. Lewis is removing the bounty."

"That suits me," Turner said, mopping his brow with a handkerchief.

"No chance he'll change his mind?" Archer asked.

"I doubt it," Detmer said. "Somethin' you two said to him last night got to him. About his granddaughter. He even asked me to be her guardian if he died before finding someone to take care of her. So I'm stayin' on."

"What do you say?" Archer asked Roxy.

"I say we get on our horses and get the hell out of town!"

They stepped out of the bank, and not a shot was fired. All the men watched them walk off toward the livery.

LADY GUNSMITH
BOOKS 1 - 9

AWARD-WINNING AUTHOR
ROBERT J. RANDISI (J.R. ROBERTS)

ANGEL EYES SERIES

For more information
visit: www.SpeakingVolumes.us

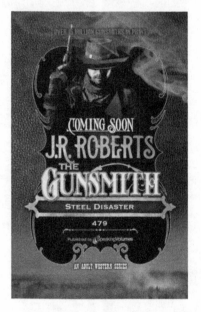

J.R. ROBERTS

THE GUNSMITH
BOOKS 430 – 478

**For more information
visit:** <u>www.SpeakingVolumes.us</u>

J.R. ROBERTS

THE GUNSMITH GIANT SERIES

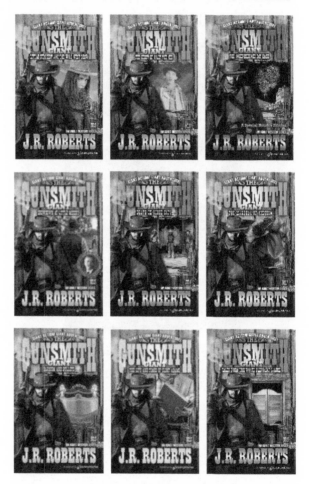

Sign up for free and bargain books

Join the Speaking Volumes mailing list

Text

ILOVEBOOKS

to 22828 to get started.

Message and data rates may apply.

Made in United States
North Haven, CT
03 October 2022

24952741R00136